BLOOD VIRTUE

THE SEARCHERS
BOOK THREE

JESSICA MARTING

SHADOW PRESS

BLOOD VIRTUE

Blood Virtue (The Searchers Book 3)

ISBN 978-1-989780-30-5

Second Edition

This book was originally published by Evernight Publishing with the title *The Falls*. It was been revised, expanded, and re-edited.

For David.

CHAPTER
ONE

8 November, 1889

S eecombe,

    Please find enclosed the wedding invitation my fiancée and the rest of the Searchers felt appropriate to send to you. Whether you choose to attend or not has no bearing on our future happiness; rather the newly appointed lieutenant of the New York branch of the Searchers was the person responsible for our extending the invitation. Miss Violet Singer felt it prudent given your role in the Mayfair incident last spring, and she is curious to meet one of her British counterparts.

    You will treat Miss Singer and the future Mrs. Sterling with the utmost of respect, lest I demonstrate my improved performance with stake and mallet upon your person.

    We anticipate your presence on the 29th of December.

Maximilian Sterling

~

SAMUEL'S TEETH chattered on the open observation deck of the dirigible. He had to remind himself to breathe in the frigid air. The massive aircraft moved with such speed that he swore he could feel tiny invisible icicles pricking at his eyes, his nose, every bit of exposed skin.

Bloody hell, how could people live in such climates? And why had he ventured to the open deck again?

He remembered the heavy, cloying stink of cigar and pipe smoke in the upper-class lounge and shuddered. *That* was why he wandered out here. Mingling among the other passengers had become unbearable. It was an unspeakable choice, really: freeze his arse off on the open deck of a dirigible crossing the Atlantic Ocean in late December or sit among noxious fumes and make aggravating small talk with those responsible for the fumes in the first place. If he thought he could get away with it, Samuel might have taken his chances getting some air, albeit stuffy and stale, in the steam class lounge, but was certain he would be chased out as soon as those passengers saw him or heard his Mayfair accent. Returning to his cramped cabin was unthinkable, since the smells had reached it, too, permeating the walls and bedding.

This was untenable. Samuel officially loathed traveling by air.

Breathe in, breathe out. Appreciate the clean scent outdoors and ignore the chill.

He couldn't believe people actually paid to go to Swiss vitality clinics for the cold mountain air.

Breathe in, breathe out. Ignore the icicles forming in your nostrils.

He fumbled through his traveling satchel for his box camera and raised it to the deck railing. The light was bright enough for the device to capture images, although he could only guess whether it would correctly focus on the frigid ocean waves roiling beneath the dirigible. He'd find out once he landed in New York, took all the pictures the camera could, and then send his camera to the Kodak plant to have the film processed. That was the best and worst part of his new hobby, the waiting and then seeing what he'd managed to capture on film.

He was the lone passenger on the open deck, save for one of the dirigible's poor stewards who now briskly walked to him, seemingly impervious to the cold. "Can I get you something to warm you up, sir?" The man's American twang was unmistakable, his expression friendly. "A hot toddy or a cigar, maybe?"

Samuel needed to get used to that, given his impending stay in America. He shuddered faintly in revulsion at the idea of cigar smoke, let alone smoking one. "A toddy," he said shortly, then remembered the man wasn't a servant in the British sense. This was an American dirigible with American employees. He quickly corrected himself. "A hot toddy, please."

"Right away, sir. You'll still be here?"

"I will."

The steward pointed to his camera, still in Samuel's gloved hands. "What's that, if you don't mind my asking?"

"It's a box camera."

"A *camera*? Well, they're just getting smaller and smaller, aren't they?" The steward smiled. "I'll be back with your drink in a couple of minutes, sir."

"Thank you."

He was getting better at remembering to say

please and thank you to the help. Ada Burgess, soon to be Ada Sterling, might be pleased about that. If nothing else, Samuel was determined to adhere to American customs while he was abroad. It was the polite thing to do.

He wouldn't even concern himself with what her fiancé would think of his attempt at cultivating American manners. Samuel was certain that Maximilian Sterling would never, ever care for him.

The steward returned with a steaming cup and presented it to Samuel, who thanked him and took a sip.

Oh, dear God.

He tried not to make a face at the taste, but the steward noticed something was amiss. "Is something wrong, sir?"

"No," Samuel said. Damn it, he would be *polite*. "May I ask what this is made with?"

"Only the finest bourbon, sir. The best Tennessee has to offer."

Bourbon. Was this what American distilleries could produce? Samuel made a point to remain sober during his time in America. "Very good," he said. "I shall enjoy it."

He would enjoy the hot toddy, damn it, just as he would enjoy New York City.

~

"You don't have to go out of your way to aid Mr. Seecombe, Violet," said Max. "I'm certain he can navigate the New York Airfield on his own."

"What kind of host are you, anyway?" Violet wrapped herself in her heavy winter coat.

"The kind of host who isn't boarding Samuel

Seecombe in my home. My offer to pay for his hotel stay still stands."

"And that's where your being ungracious ends," his fiancée, Ada, said. "We talked about this already. Samuel helped save my bacon back in London, and the least we could do is invite him to our wedding."

"Actually, he's invited because we all agreed we need to increase our lines of communication with the rest of the world," Violet said by way of correction. "Inviting him to a social occasion is good manners, and if he's as stiff and proper as you've told me, he won't cause a scene or embarrass anyone." Coat buttoned and voluminous knitted scarf wound around her neck, she looked around her flat one last time. It was tidy, just as she liked it, and ready to welcome her new boarder. The room Samuel Seecombe would stay in was ready to receive its visitor. "He also would have received the cable I sent before he left London. He'll be expecting me." Violet was looking forward to having a guest, besides. She enjoyed having company.

Ada and Max were likewise putting on their winter coats, although they wouldn't be accompanying her to the airfield to meet Mr. Seecombe. "Please tell me you're not planning on going out to hunt tonight. Me, Max, and Frank have our part of Brooklyn taken care of," Ada said.

Between Ada and her brother, and her husband-to-be, their Brooklyn territory would be well cared for, should any vampires be stupid enough try to make a home there. "I'm staying in. I take full advantage of my nights off now. I have enough work during the day to ensure I don't have the energy to take on extra shifts at night."

"Keep on doing that. But I still miss working with you in the field, you know."

As the new lieutenant of the New York branch of the Searchers, Violet found she was doing more work during the day than she'd ever thought possible. It was wreaking havoc on her sleep. She wouldn't trust herself to hunt vampires right now, anyway. She was likely to get bitten or worse when she was tired.

But she wasn't so tired she couldn't go to the airfield. Max and Ada followed her out of her flat, and Violet locked the door behind them. Once outside, she hailed a steam cab and climbed in. "I'll see you tomorrow morning at headquarters," she said before she closed the cab door.

"We'll have a full report at the ready," Ada promised.

Violet smiled and closed the door, and she heard Max bidding her goodbye and good luck through the vehicle as he hailed a steam cab for the two of them.

"Where to?" the driver asked.

"The airfield, please."

"New York or Coney Island?" He sounded irritated at the request.

The Coney Island Airfield had opened just a couple of weeks ago. Ada's brothers had picked up work there during its construction. Violet had completely forgotten about it. "New York."

"New York it is."

Violet settled back on the cab's stained cloth seat and tried to ignore the cold December wind whistling through cracks in the window. A couple of hot bricks, wrapped in dirty flannel, rested on the cab floor and she put her feet on them. She watched the city through the grimy glass as afternoon shifted into twilight. She was glad she wasn't scheduled to go out hunting tonight, not that her vampire sense was picking up any bloodsuckers nearby. Vampire activity had dimmed in recent months in New York thanks to the countless hours put in by the Searchers.

The steam cab left her outside the airfield and Violet braced herself against the cold before walking through its gates. Samuel Seecombe was scheduled to arrive on the *Hope*, an American-owned dirigible, at half past five. Checking the pocket watch she always carried, she saw it should be landing any minute, and she hurried through the ever-present crowds to the docks.

She had little to go on as to what to look for. Ada had described Samuel Seecombe as a "stuffy, prissy upper-class bastard in clothing nicer than he was," and she wasn't sure how she could pinpoint those qualities in a traveler. Max had been a little more helpful, telling her to look for a tall, fair-skinned man in his early thirties with dark hair and blue eyes, but Ada was still sure that would de-scribe many of the passengers disembarking from the *Hope*. She'd sent a cable to the London branch before he was scheduled to depart, asking him to meet her and telling him to look for a silver-haired woman wearing a thick blue knitted scarf and matching hat. There was no point in beating about the bush when it came her crowning glory, only blond and magnificent until she was twenty, ten years' prior. Silver-haired, not gray. Gray hair de-noted someone much older than she was.

Remembering that cable, she looked around the other people waiting for the *Hope* to finish docking. She was the only silver-haired woman wearing a blue scarf and hat that she could see.

The wind shifted a little in the outdoor waiting area, and she stuffed her mittened hands in her coat pockets, looking up to see the huge shape of the *Hope* begin its descent. Its anchors dropped, and airfield workers quickly rushed to secure them to pulleys that would drag the dirigible out of the sky. It was fascinating to watch, a sight Violet rarely got to take it. She hardly traveled, let alone on a dirigible.

The dirigible secured, passengers started walking down the dock's gangplanks, luggage in hand. Violet kept her gaze fixed on the people disembarking, looking for a single man who matched Max and Ada's vague descriptions. She wished she asked the London branch to provide a better description of her guest.

A mix of accents and languages greeted her ears as passengers greeted and mingled with the people waiting for them. Violet fidgeted impatiently as the minutes ticked past. Was Samuel Seecombe looking for her as well, or had he decided to simply take off and make his way to her flat on his own? She didn't know what to expect.

Finally, an unaccompanied man walked down the gangplank. Tall, dark-haired, about her age, impeccably dressed in a fine coat, bulging satchel over one shoulder and large valise in hand. The look of uncertainty flitting across his face sparked a flare of hope in Violet. Maybe this was the man she was looking for.

She pushed her way through the crowd until she was at the foot of the gangplank. Snowflakes swirled in the air, settling on his coat. "Mr. Seecombe?" she said.

He looked at her and started. "Yes?"

Violet held out one of her hands. "Violet Singer."

He stared at her hand for a moment, then her, before gingerly accepting it and shaking her hand. "Welcome to New York, Mr. Seecombe," Violet said.

"Thank you."

She could tell he was trying not to show it, but he must be freezing cold. "I sent a cable before you were scheduled to leave London. I have a room ready at my flat if you're inclined to stay there." And why wouldn't he? It was free rent for him.

He continued to look at her quizzically.

"Unless you'd prefer to stay at a hotel," she said.

"No, I appreciate your hospitality," he replied.

The strange look he gave her only waned slightly. Violet took that a sign of encouragement. Ada had warned her before that Mr. Seecombe seemed to have some peculiar and archaic attitudes about women working as vampire hunters. She hoped she wasn't making a mistake by letting him stay at her flat. But some Searcher traditions were still adhered to, even in America. And one of them was extending invitations to hunters visiting from overseas.

"Well then, you must be tired and hungry from your trip," Violet said. "It's a short walk back to the street, and we'll take a steam cab home."

"Thank you."

Mr. Seecombe was quiet while they threaded their way through the crowds to the street. Violet sneaked the occasional look at him. He looked a little bewildered, out of his element, and not bearing a trace of the arrogance Ada and Max had complained about.

But then, they'd barely spoken ten words between them so far. And he could be too tired or hungry to be difficult right now. Or polite. The English were crazy about manners, according to Ada.

She hailed a steam cab and it clattered to the curb. "Don't expect the driver to help with your things," Violet said, opening the cab's back door.

Mr. Seecombe looked surprised at the gesture. "After you," he said.

Violet stepped in and slid down the seat, and he followed, setting his satchel between them and the valise at his feet. Unlike the one that brought her to the airfield, this cab didn't have heated bricks on the floor, nor did the driver greet them beyond asking for their destination.

"I would like to tell you that drivers are better mannered than this, but I would be lying," Violet said quietly.

A tiny smile quirked at the corners of Mr. Seecombe's mouth, and some of the chill around him thawed a little.

"My apologies, Mrs. Singer," he said.

"Miss. And please call me Violet." Would he extend the same invitation to use his first name?

"I must admit that based on the description in the cable you sent, I was expecting someone else."

"Someone older," she said.

"Yes." He paused. "Please call me Samuel."

MISS SINGER—*VIOLET*, Samuel corrected himself —lived in a surprisingly spacious flat, nicely decorated in dark, masculine colors and full of the modern conveniences that he hadn't expected to see in America. Vampire hunting wasn't an especially well-paying job, but in England at least the Searchers tended to be from the upper classes, making money less of an issue. Part of him was dying to ask how an unmarried, female Searcher could maintain such a space, but even in looser American conversation he knew that would be unwelcomed.

Violet unwound her voluminous scarf and took off her heavy coat and hat, revealing a dark gray skirt and bright blue shirtwaist. A thin silver chain was looped around her throat, a small cross dangling from it. It was a defense against vampires that managed to be both practical and sophisticated, as was the big silver clip resting in her matching hair, pinned on top of her head, a few loose curls escaping to frame her face.

She had to be the most unusual-looking woman Samuel had ever seen. Unusual and attractive, and he would *not* let himself stare at her.

He realized she didn't have any live-in staff when she took his coat from him and stashed it in a closet. "Let me show you your room," she said, "Then I can make something for supper, if you're hungry."

He was. The memory of that awful bourbon hot toddy sent a wave of revulsion through him. Coupled with his body being out of sorts with the shift from London time to New York's, he was wearier than he'd felt in years. "Much appreciated, thanks," he said.

She led him down a short corridor and opened the door to his bedroom. Like the rest of the flat, it was tastefully decorated in dark, muted colors. Judging from the bright color of her blouse, it hadn't been her who had done the decorating. It was one more thing he wanted to ask her about.

"Make yourself at home," she said. "I'm going to make something for us, and I'm sure you have some questions."

Had she read his mind? Did American Searchers have that ability alongside the vampire sense that called them into service?

But her expression remained friendly, green eyes sparkling. Samuel nodded, and Violet left him, returning to the kitchen.

He unpacked his satchel first, setting his box camera on top of the highboy, and examined the clothing he'd brought with him. The garments he planned to wear to Max Sterling and Ada Burgess's wedding were wrinkled, but it was nothing a good steam couldn't take care of. Violet was sure to have a steamer somewhere in here, although he would probably have to press them himself. Unless Violet had a housekeeper, which guessing from the size of the flat was a possibility. Was it customary for Americans to hang their own clothes? It probably was.

Damn it, he was out of his element. It wasn't a feeling he was accustomed to, and he hated it. It was the biggest reason he avoided leaving London as much as possible. He couldn't understand Max Sterling's affinity for taking off for parts unknown for months or years at a time. He looked at the bed longingly, already eager to get some much-needed rest, but that would have to wait.

He found Violet ladling a rich-smelling stew into bowls at a beautifully set table. Electric lamps cast a warm glow over the room and her, who smiled at him. "My apologies. This probably isn't what you're used to," she said. "I rarely have the chance to play hostess, nor do I have a cook. Would you care for some wine?"

"Please."

They sat down opposite one another, and Samuel resisted the urge to wolf down his food.

"How was your journey?" Violet asked.

"Chilly." The response was automatic. He didn't think she would mind if he complained a little about the cold, but he didn't want to start whining this early in their acquaintance. He continued, "Not entirely unpleasant, but the lounges and staterooms smelled terribly of tobacco."

"You don't indulge, I assume?"

"I can't abide the odor."

"Then we should get on just fine," Violet said. "I don't tolerate smoking in my flat or inside the Searcher headquarters, even if my housekeeper wouldn't entertain notions of killing me if I did."

At the mention of headquarters, Samuel remembered her recent promotion. "Congratulations on your new post, by the way."

"Thank you." She beamed at him from across the table. "Though I should warn you that nepotism worked in my favor, and I'm only lieutenant temporarily. My uncle is head of the New York branch. I've already told him that I prefer to be in the field instead of behind a desk." She took a delicate sip of wine. "I'm told the London branch is still strictly male."

He felt himself color a little, remembering how he must have come across to Ada Burgess at their first meeting at Seven Sisters railway station, so many months ago. "I understand that we're regarded as Neanderthals for that reason. Although I should tell you that Miss Burgess's visit has sparked some conversation about the need for change."

Although it wasn't just Miss Burgess, he thought. It was Bert Radcliffe's death, too. But thinking about Ada Burgess didn't make him sick with guilt the way Radcliffe did.

"I'm pleased to hear that. It's time for England to catch up to the rest of the world."

"I don't know if that's possible, actually," he said. "There were women with the vampire sense, but they were kept in the dark about what it meant."

"So they never joined the Searchers, didn't marry and have children with our men…"

"And the men who were Searchers didn't tell their daughters if they inherited it, either," Samuel said. He braced himself to tell her the bad news. "They died out. *We're* dying out."

But she didn't seem surprised to hear that. "Ada guessed as much."

Of course she had. Ada was bright, brave, and very good at her job from what he'd gleaned from Searchers intelligence. She and Max had been taken by surprise the previous spring by a young vampire who bore terrifying strength for his age; it happened occasionally. More often than not these days, the hunters were the victors, although it had been a close shave for Ada.

Radcliffe hadn't been so lucky.

Don't think about him right now!

"Our problem is one of the reasons I came to America," he said. Seeing Violet's widened eyes, he realized how that could be construed and quickly tried to explain himself better. "I'm not viewing that as a potential solution." He wasn't here to try to arrange marriages between female American Searchers and British men, but to learn from the American methods. "You've hired Searchers without the sense to expand your ranks. We all know the vampire problem is getting worse with the advent of mass transportation."

"Are you telling me there was a vampire onboard the *Hope*?"

"No. But as vampires turn more and more to their side, we have to come up with better ways to combat it without the public at large finding out and causing mass hysteria."

"Again."

"Exactly." Violet had likely heard the same stories as Samuel, as had everyone else in the world. Only the Searchers knew they were true and monsters walked among them. They'd managed to keep vampires' existence secret since the Middle Ages, and it wasn't easy. "Part of my reason for accepting the wedding invitation is to see how you operate on this side of the pond."

"I'm always happy to help in that regard." She changed the subject. "Max and Ada's wedding is in three days' time. Is there anything else you would like to do while you're in New York until then?"

"Make myself useful."

Violet's eyes sparkled at his answer, and a wicked grin spread across her face. She really was enchanting, Samuel thought. Her unusual hair shining in the lamplight made her look like a fairy from one of the stories his governess read him as a child. Albeit very deadly fairy, he reminded himself.

"Would you like to take a night shift or two while you're here?"

He did. He needed a shift that wasn't in London, bringing back awful memories. "I brought my best stake and mallet with me. I wouldn't dream of taking anything less than a working holiday."

That earned another smile from her. "As long as we're both in one piece before the wedding. Ada will be very upset if I'm not there."

~

ADA'S russet hair was artfully arranged on top of her head, curls already escaping from their pins. Her light gray gown fit her perfectly, the same color as her bridegroom's shirt. Both of them wore radiant smiles as they made the short walk down the aisle to the church's entrance, Ada's brothers and sisters-in-law trailing them.

It was a small wedding party, uncharacteristic of a wedding to which nearly every vampire hunter on the east coast had been invited. Violet recognized everyone and noted that everyone in attendance had to be concealing wooden stakes and mallets, just in case. A supper was scheduled to be held right after the ceremony that would doubtlessly continue late into the night, and it never hurt to be prepared. She was sure that Max and Ada themselves had to armed with at least some holy water.

Samuel had surprised her and Ada when he offered to snap a few photographs with his box camera a couple of nights ago. Their initial meeting at headquarters had been frosty, until Samuel offered a sincere apology for his behavior in London and an offer of being an unofficial wedding photographer.

The wedding supper was held at Violet's uncle's house, a huge monstrosity that kept the neighbors talking thanks to its fortifications against vampires. Angus Singer's home had crucifixes in every window, strips of silver nailed to every sill and doorway, and a lingering smell of garlic hung in the air even though he'd taken down the bulbs he usually kept at each entrance. But no one seemed to care about the smell tonight; this was an evening for celebration.

Violet waded her way through the crowd, half of whom were already well on their way to being sauced despite supper not yet having been served. She spotted Samuel with his camera, snapping a photo of Edgar and Molly Burgess in front of an electric lamp. She heard him to trying to explain that he needed as much light as possible to get their image to show up on film, then some technical words about photography that went right over Violet's head. It seemed to fly over Edgar and Molly's as well, but they obliged, moving a little closer to the light source.

But talking about his hobby seemed to bring out the first genuine smiles she had seen from him since his arrival in New York. His face lit up as brightly as the lamps as he explained how the image was made on the film and how it would be processed. He promised to send them the photographs after he had them made. Developed, Violet noted. Photographs were developed.

There was hardly a shred of the snobby man Ada had described so vividly when she returned from London. Maybe he had just needed a change of scenery. God knew she could use one.

She didn't realize she was staring at Samuel until a nudge on her shoulder snapped her out of it. "Wish I saw that side of him in London," said a familiar voice.

She turned around to see Ada, more curls having escaped their pins, but she wouldn't be Adaline Burgess—no, Adaline *Sterling*—if she didn't look at least a little disheveled. It was part of her charm. "I've seen very little of the obstinate man you met in England."

It was true. He had been the politest house-guests she could hope for, and even went out with a team to Coney Island to look for a vampire sensed in the area the night before. The bloodsucker was gone by the time the Searcher team arrived, but he still tried.

"Obstinate?" Ada said. "That's a nice way of describing him."

"Difficult."

"Even nicer." She looked across the room at her new husband, now speaking to Edgar and Samuel. Max was a little more relaxed around Samuel when Edgar or Francis, Ada's brothers, was present. He caught her eye and winked, a gesture Ada returned.

Ada looped one grey-clad arm around Violet's. "We were thinking of changing our honeymoon plans to go to Niagara Falls," she said conspiratorially.

"It's the most romantic spot I can think of right now."

"Not for that. Didn't you see the cables this morning?"

"Why were you checking the cables at head-quarters on your *wedding day*?"

Ada shrugged. "We like to be prepared. There are reports of a possible vampire nest on the Canadian side, and Max and I were thinking of inves-tigating."

"What... no, Ada. Absolutely not. I forbid it."

"You can't do that!"

"I'm lieutenant, Ada. I can." Arm-in-arm, they walked through the mansion's great room, greeting guests and saying hello to Searchers from New Jersey and Connecticut. "You and Max should take a proper honeymoon. Stick to your original plans and take that trip to Venice. I'm sure there are undead to stake in Italy, and Max is arranging more flying lessons for you while you're there, anyway."

"The Canadians could use the help."

An idea struck Violet. "I'll go."

Ada swatted her arm with her free hand. "You're the lieutenant, remember?"

"And I miss being in the field. I've already told Uncle Angus I don't want the position. And again, Ada, why are you thinking about this on your *wedding day*?"

"Because this is what I do, Violet." She scanned the room, smiled at the faces of dozens of Searchers present for supper. "As soon as I mentioned it, you volunteered to go. It's what we all do. It's why everyone here, including me, is armed."

Violet leaned down enough to whisper in her friend's ear. "I was wondering where your stake and mallet are hidden."

"They're strapped to my legs." Ada's dark eyes met hers, the usual mischief in them. "Vampires don't care about weddings."

~

It was well after midnight when the wedding guests dispersed from Angus Singer's home. Violet and Samuel shared a steam cab back to Violet's flat, and she mulled over the possible trip to Niagara Falls.

She *needed* to get back to the field. Angus knew she hated being in charge and even though she wasn't gauche enough to resign at the wedding of one of her best friends, he had to know it was coming. Francis Burgess would probably make a better lieutenant; he and his wife had recently had their first child and he'd mentioned before that he wanted to be in the field a little less. Like the Singers, the Burgesses were descended from dhampirs, the human-vampire hybrids that possessed the monster-detecting sense. Frank would be a fine commander. Someday, his little daughter might be an equally fine Searcher, but that was too far off to think about.

"You're very quiet this evening," Samuel said from next to her.

"It's been a long night. Did you snap all of your pictures?" She gestured to the box camera in his lap.

"Yes."

"How many can that thing take, anyway?"

"One hundred, then I have to send the camera away to Kodak to develop the photos. They'll send it back full of new film. It's much tidier than daguerreotypes."

Violet nodded, trying to figure out how to segue the conversation to further travel. What would be the best way to propose her idea to him?

She may as well be blunt. "Samuel, what would you say to a side trip to Niagara Falls while you're on this side of the Atlantic?"

She could see surprise flit across his face in the dim light. "I would say that sounds like an adventure."

She smiled. "That's wonderful, because I've heard the Canadians need some help over there."

TWO

The dirigible that would take them to Niagara Falls was much smaller than the one that brought him to America, and mercifully, smelled decent in the lounge below decks. There wasn't any separation of the classes here, so everyone was equally uncomfortable.

They landed at a tiny, crowded airfield on the American side of Niagara Falls, then waited in line for a steam-powered trolley to take them to Canada. It was little more than a cart, just as cramped as the dirigible's lounge, but neither Samuel nor Violet complained. Samuel didn't dare, anyway. This was part of the whole adventure, every freezing moment of it.

Still, he was glad when he and Violet were admitted across the border and could leave the crowded trolley station. "We're looking for a Canadian Searcher named Frederick Lambert," she said. "I've met him before. I… oh!" She waved.

A tall figure, bedecked in heavy coat and boots, bowler hat pulled low on his forehead, walked toward them. He lifted his head and smiled at Violet.

"Frederick," she said. "It's good to see you."

He wrapped her up in a hug, not caring that they were in public. "Likewise," he said. There was an odd lilt to his accent, and Samuel guessed he was probably from a French-speaking area. Lambert turned to Samuel and stuck out a gloved hand. "Fred Lambert. I take it you're the Brit?"

The Brit. Samuel forced a smile to his face and accepted the man's proffered hand. "Samuel Seecombe, out of London."

"How's the weather treating you?" Lambert picked up Violet's oversized bag without asking or being prompted and led through the snowy street away from the station.

"It's certainly a change."

"It's a dry cold, so it isn't too bad. You'll get used to it."

Both of them easily kept up with the Canadian man's long strides. Samuel took great care on the slippery streets, unused to the ice and snow that was so much more plentiful than in New York City. "You're booked at The Guild under the names Mr. and Mrs. Seecombe," Lambert said. "The Guild doesn't let rooms to unmarried couples, and it's the only hotel in town that still had vacancies. There's a big hot air balloon show coming up soon and people are here to see it."

That comment earned an eye roll from Violet, and Samuel's gut clenched. He was not prepared to share a room with her or anyone. It just wasn't done. Even London hotels weren't that stringent about couples being married.

"How's that sound to you?" Lambert asked.

"It's fine, and we appreciate the trouble you've gone to for us," Violet said before Samuel could reply.

Lambert's expression turned grave and he lowered his voice. "It's bad here, Violet. We've never had enough of a problem with the bloodsuckers before that we needed outside help." He held out his free gloved hand, as if in bewilderment. "We've never needed to have full time Searchers here. They couldn't be bothered to come all the way up here, since it's too cold and there's not enough people to eat or turn without others noticing. Now there's a bunch of them just hanging out here, and they're bound to go farther north. The Montreal branch sent me here two weeks ago, and I've been busy almost every night." He sighed. "I'm exhausted. We all are. And we really appreciate your help."

"Let us get settled into the hotel and you'll tell us everything," Violet said.

"Let me feed you, too. I can't imagine the dirigible food is any good."

"Food?" Samuel said. "We were supposed to be fed?"

That remark earned a smile from Violet, and despite the seriousness of the vampire problem ahead of them, he couldn't keep a tiny bubble of happiness from welling up in him at the sight.

THE ROOM BOOKED for Samuel and Violet was tidy and clean, well-appointed without being too fussy. It reminded Violet of the decorating scheme in her own home, one she hadn't chosen but didn't see the point in changing after she took it over. She and Samuel put their things away, then left the room to meet with Fred Lambert in the hotel's restaurant. She didn't know about Fred or Samuel, but Violet could certainly use a decent hot meal following their voyage.

The restaurant was sparsely populated this early in the afternoon, and Lambert already waited for them at a corner table, as far away from the other patrons as possible. "I took the liberty of requesting steak pie for all of us," he said, nodding at the plates set around the table. "Best thing they can make here. That all right?"

The gesture irked Violet a little, and a quick glance at Samuel and the set line of his mouth told her he likely felt the same. Still, it was kind, and the Canadian branches were paying for their stay here, anyway. "That's fine," she said, letting Samuel pull out her chair for her. She sat down and he did likewise next to her.

A brief silence fell over the table as she and Samuel tasted their steak pie. It was hot and edible, and that's what mattered to Violet at that moment. Finally, she said, "Tell us about the problem here."

"It's worse closer to the border," Lambert said. "Toronto and Montreal usually see the most of them, since there are so many people there, but it's still manageable. Maybe two or three bloodsuckers a week. It's just too goddamn cold for them to go anywhere else."

"Vampires don't usually care about the weather," Samuel said.

"True, but living people do," Lambert said. "I'm not sure what the winter's like in England, but this time of year is so cold no one leaves the house if they can help it." He took a forkful of steak pie and swallowed it before speaking again. "If no one leaves the house…"

Samuel finished for him. "And no one invites them in, vampires can't eat anyone."

"You got it. We have Searchers still hunting in the cities, but we really needed help here. They're coming over the border in record numbers. Staked three in as many days. Three! I'd usually get three over six or seven weeks in Montreal."

"They're running out of places to feed without fear in America," Violet said. "They know we're after them."

Lambert nodded. "That's what we guessed. Damned stupid of us that we never thought they might run out of places to hide, but…" He held out his hands as if in defeat. "Here we are."

"So where should Mr. Seecombe and I start looking?" Violet asked. "All we need is a decent sleep this afternoon and some territory. We're both…" She paused as a well-dressed man walked past their table, lowering her voice before she spoke again. "We're both experienced hunters with the sense, we should be able to put a big dent in the problem."

"That's the thing," Lambert said. "It's too difficult to hunt discreetly here. Niagara Falls never really sleeps."

Samuel gave him a look that clearly questioned his intelligence, and Violet knew she wore a matching expression. "Mr. Lambert…"

"Fred."

"Fred, then. With respect, Miss Singer is from New York. I'm from London. Both are cities in states of perpetual wakefulness."

Now it was Lambert's turn to look irritated. "Montreal isn't *that* rural."

The last thing—all right, the *second* to last thing, after being bitten by a vampire—that Violet wanted was to deal with a pissing match between Samuel and Lambert.

The two stared daggers at each other, and Violet sighed. She was lieutenant of the New York branch; defusing tension was part of her job now. "Comparisons between our respective cities' nightlife won't get us anywhere," she said. "Fred, please continue."

If Samuel's feathers were ruffled at this, the Englishman didn't let on.

"As I was saying, Niagara Falls is a big city in a small town. There's always something happening," Lambert said. "At the moment, it's the hot air balloon show in town and that house that's supposed to be haunted. Big crowds in a small space. And everyone knows each other, and the vampires know that."

"So others notice when someone goes missing," Samuel said.

"Now you're getting it. You can't live in a town with a population this size and not have friends and acquaintances who would notice you missing. And that's one of the reasons we sent New York a cable about this."

"Missing persons?" Violet asked.

"No, they turned up. Two frozen bodies left on Goat Island a month ago, before I arrived. Did you hear about that, Violet? Goat Island is technically in the New York branch's jurisdiction."

It pained Violet to admit that she didn't know about that incident, even though Fred Lambert was incorrect about it being part of her territory. "I work with the New York City limits," she said. "Niagara Falls is under the New York State territory. Vampires aren't as plentiful in the rural areas as they are in the boroughs."

"Well, they weren't like the bodies vampires usually leave behind," Lambert said. "Two men, later identified as being brothers from Niagara Falls, reported missing by their sister two weeks before. One had his throat ripped out. The other was burned-up ash beside him inside his clothes. There was a two-man ornithopter crashed near the bodies. That's the only way someone's getting to Goat Island this time of year."

"One was a vampire, the other tried to eat him," Samuel said.

"That's what it looks like. One brother turned, lures him out to eat his brother. Or the brother wants to be turned, who the hell knows. They were walking around in daylight just fine before they went missing, so the vampire brother was obviously recently turned. He wouldn't have been out past dawn if that wasn't the case. That flying machine was a recent model, too. Expensive. He still had the bill of sale crumpled up in his coat pocket.

"Two drained bodies showed up a couple of miles north of here," Lambert continued. "That's when some of us from the major cities decided to investigate, and by some of us, I mean me. And this is more than I know what to handle. Like I said, I deal with three vampire attacks in six weeks in Montreal. There are only so many places I can think of to look for these bastards without asking for help."

"What about your sense?" Samuel asked.

"That's the thing," Lambert said. "It's giving me a hell of a headache nearly every time the sun goes down, stronger than I've ever felt at home. Niagara Falls may very well be crawling with vampires for all I know, and I can hardly track all them down on my own."

～

Samuel kept his admittedly low opinion of the Canadian Searcher to himself until he and Violet returned to their room.

"This is unbelievable," he said, looking out the window at the snowy street outside. "How can you sense vampires and be unable to find them? That's why we become Searchers in the first place."

"I'm as confused as you are," Violet said. "And I think we should be grateful that they asked for help. If Fred Lambert is only staking a vampire or two each month, it explains why he and the rest of his countrymen are so befuddled. We're both used to staking at least a couple every week." She looked around the room. "I don't know about you, but I'm going to get some sleep before we start working tonight."

"That's a good idea."

She fixed her green eyes on him. "I prefer to sleep in a night dress," she said.

"I imagine it's more comfortable that way."

She sighed, but there was a ghost of a smile on her lips. "Samuel, I have to get undressed."

It finally hit him. "Oh! Shall I leave the room?"

"And let the hotel staff know we're not married? No, just turn around, please." There was a teasing note to her voice, one he rarely heard from others. He liked it.

"Our wandering about in the middle of the night won't rouse suspicions?" He turned around and fussed with the heavy window draperies, pulling them closed. Darkness descended on the room, and Samuel blinked at the change.

"If anyone asks, we're out to look at that haunted house Mr. Lambert mentioned."

"How will you explain the differences in our accents?" He heard the rustle of fabric as she changed into her nightclothes. An image popped into his mind of what she might look like undressed, and he closed his eyes, willing it away. This was a situation that was already awkward without adding that to the mix.

"It's simple. You took a trip to New York for some reason or another, fell in love with me and the city, and stayed."

Samuel didn't know how to describe how he felt hearing those words. He was fairly certain he'd never been in love before, and the idea of that happening seemed so farfetched as to be impossible, let alone with a woman like Violet Singer. But that was the last thing he would tell her. Instead, he said, "You didn't take a holiday to London and become enamoured with it and me?"

"Well, no. I've never been, so I couldn't describe it as well as you could New York. You can turn around now."

He did, and through the darkness saw she had changed into a plain nightdress and was now braiding her long silver hair. "I'd offer to sleep on the divan, but there isn't one," she said. "I don't mind sharing the bed. I've had to do it on missions before."

For some reason, it rankled Samuel that she'd done that, and he had no right to feel that way.

"Are you going to get some sleep, too?" she asked.

He nodded stiffly. "Yes."

She turned on her side, away from him, offering some privacy. Samuel quickly shucked his clothes and changed into a set of nightclothes, something he never wore at home but knew was appropriate here.

"I wish I'd thought to bring a bottle of whisky

with me. I could use a nightcap," he said. He remembered the horrible hot toddy he'd choked down on the dirigible to New York and suppressed a shudder.

"Me, too." She turned over to face him. "I really do appreciate your taking the time to come here, you know. You could have just returned to London after Max and Ada's wedding."

"And miss the opportunity to stake vampires in another country? Not to mention another stamp on my passport?"

He heard the smile in her voice. "You really aren't as bad as Ada made you out to be."

A twinge of shame and embarrassment washed over Samuel, not for the first time since he'd landed on this side of the Atlantic. "I was an ass when we met," he said. "I'm actively working on not being an ass now."

There was also the matter of what happened with Radcliffe last autumn. It wasn't something he wanted to discuss yet, even with someone as understanding as Violet.

"You haven't been one at all since I met you at the airfield."

"It isn't much of an excuse, but when I met her and Mr. Sterling at the railway station, I was just so surprised to see her," he said. "I've told you that the British branches haven't been very modern in allowing women to work with us, and it's to our detriment. It was a surprise to see an unmarried American woman traveling alone, working as a Searcher, and then to find out she's actually very good at the job. It was a shock."

"You really need to catch up on modern times, Sam. Can I call you Sam?"

"I don't see the harm."

"Good." She snuggled in deeper under the blankets, fluffing the pillow under her head. "Can your camera take good photographs in the dark? I saw you had some trouble at the wedding."

"I need as much light as possible for the best photographs, but it can still be done. I can experiment when I get my camera back from the Kodak plant." He would be able to retrieve it when they returned to New York. He wished now that he'd known about this trip in advance so he could have saved some film for it.

"Have you ever taken a photograph of a vampire?"

Samuel stilled. "No."

"Do you know if the rumors are true that they can't be photographed? As far as I know, no one's tried in New York."

"Well, they don't tend to stay put in one place very long."

"I'd like to see if that's true," Violet said.

"Are you proposing that I approach a vampire and explain that I would like to try to take his photograph before I stake him?"

"No." There was that smile again. "But suppose you sense one in a crowd before he senses you. It wouldn't hurt to try."

"Subjects have to remain perfectly still," he said. Her face fell. "But I still would have liked to have taken some of the waterfalls themselves. When will I get another chance to?"

And one of Violet, to remember her by.

"All right. Good night, Sam," she said.

He envied her ability to fall asleep in the middle of the afternoon with so little difficulty. He was all too aware of the warmth of her next to him, something he so rarely experienced. He wasn't sure if he liked it.

Samuel was used to being on his own. He wasn't even especially close to his Searcher colleagues. Or his parents. When it came down to it, he had no one.

He looked over at Violet's bundled-up form. From what he'd seen in New York, she appeared to have a circle of friends and acquaintances around her. She didn't bear the aura of a lonely woman. That was something else he could add to the list of things he envied about her.

Taking care not to disturb her, he rolled over on his side and tried to fall asleep.

THREE

I t was nearly eight o'clock when Samuel and Violet left the hotel, and so cold outside that even she felt it. She was pleased that Samuel had taken her advice and bundled up as much as he could, but knew the chill had to be bothering him.

Niagara Falls at night was just as alive and vibrant as it was during the day. The town's streets were illuminated by tall electric lampposts that spilled warm yellow light across the snow, and despite the incredible, bone-deep chill and lateness of the evening, vendors still sold hot drinks, including toddies. But when she offered to buy one for Samuel, he scrunched his face up like he smelled something bad and declined.

Snob, she thought, and purchased one for herself instead. But she couldn't be mad at him. Thus far, he had proven to be far less of an ingrate than Max Sterling led her to believe.

"Tennessee bourbon," Samuel said, breaking her out of her thoughts.

"I beg your pardon?"

"I don't care for what Tennessee distilleries

produce. I tried a hot toddy on the dirigible to New York. It did not sit well with me."

Violet stared at him. "Bless you, Sam."

Now it was Samuel's turn to look puzzled.

"Did you really think they would be serving American bourbon in a Canadian town? This is made with Club Whisky. You should bring a bottle back to London to show your friends." She took an appreciative swallow, enjoying the pleasant burn down her throat.

"Are you implying that Canadian whisky can hold its own over Scottish?"

She looked at him archly. "I wasn't implying anything, but I'll state it outright that Club Whisky is at least equal to Sheep Dip."

Surprise flitted across his face at her words. She hoped he wouldn't press her further. Her whisky knowledge was gleaned from her uncle's discussions about it, no more than that. For the most part, it all tasted the same to her.

He didn't. She held the cup out to him. "Want to taste?"

He accepted it from her, took a tentative sip. His expression remained neutral. "It's drinkable, although I'm obligated to point out that it's isn't on the same plane as a single malt. My apologies to the Canadian whisky distillers."

She took the drink back. "I'm sure they accept."

Samuel changed the subject. "What are the chances that we run into our friend Mr. Lambert tonight?"

"I couldn't tell you. He's hunting closer to the edge of town. We're supposed to stay with the living and try to track down any undead here."

"I gathered that before, but just how far does this town's limits extend?"

She looked up at one of the street lamps. Was that a bat she spied? No, just the light flickering. She and Samuel would have sensed a shifted vampire before they saw it, and besides, regular people would notice a bat flying through a winter night. "Are you trying to avoid him?"

"No."

There was something in his tone of voice that didn't convince Violet. "You can tell me," she said.

He was quiet for a moment, and they walked past a vendor selling something hot and savory. Violet's mouth watered, but she didn't stop. "It's not him, exactly," Samuel finally said.

"Then what is it?"

He was quiet again. Thinking, Violet knew. "It's so unorganized here," he said.

Violet wanted to laugh but knew it would be unappreciated. "I believe Ada said something to the same effect of the London branch."

"And while disorganization is one of the many problems that plagues the Searchers in that part of the world, it isn't quite as bad as this. Where are the headquarters?"

"There are two offices in Ontario, in Toronto and Ottawa. Others in Montreal, Victoria. Vampires like to travel by air, you know."

"*Four* headquarters for a country of this size." He sounded incredulous.

"A country of this size, climate, and population that doesn't see vampire activity anywhere close to the level that we do in America or England." She sighed. "Sam, I like you, but I think Ada's right about some things. You're a little..." She searched for the right words. She wasn't worried about offending or insulting him, exactly, as what she wanted to say was neither offensive nor an insult, but her words still required care.

But Samuel was the one to help her out. "Naive?"

She thought for a few seconds. "Naive, yes. That works."

"Believe it or not, I haven't traveled much in my life. I've left England a handful of times, for either France or Scotland. That's it."

Violet was genuinely surprised to hear that. "Really?"

"There wasn't much opportunity for me to travel. There were too many vampires and not enough Searchers, and my father insisted I attend university in London and live at his home."

"What did you study?"

"I beg your pardon?"

"What are you, by trade? Besides a Searcher."

"Given that I'm the son of a second son, I do have a trade, actually." It took Violet a few seconds to realize her gaffe. Samuel was part of the upper classes. There was bound to be a few noble titles in his family tree. "I'm a barrister."

"So do you handle the estates of the vampires you stake?"

"Very amusing, and no, I don't. I've only practiced law among my colleagues in the Searchers." There was a stiffness to his voice as he admitted that, and Violet knew his profession touched on a nerve.

She dared to prod further. "You don't like being a lawyer?" She quickly corrected herself. "Barrister."

"I haven't had the opportunity to practice as I trained to do, so I don't know. This has been my life since I was fifteen years old." He looked around the cold street, as if expecting a vampire to pop out of nowhere and start mauling people.

"And you're a photographer. How did you become interested in that?"

He paused, as if searching for words. "I needed a hobby."

It was a simple explanation and it made perfect sense. It was so easy to get caught up in vampire hunting, easy to forget that one was still alive and should experience life as much as possible. Violet knew, as did all Searchers, just how short and unfair life could be. It was one of the reasons she approved of Ada's European trip in the spring, why she was so happy to see her friend married to a man who knew the importance of living as well.

Violet, unlike Samuel, did not possess any hobbies at the moment. Nor lovers, but that wasn't something she would tell Samuel, although he would have likely guessed that by now. An attached woman did not share a bed with a man even if it was completely platonic.

Well, neither did unattached women, but sometimes sacrifices had to be made. She stole a glance at him. His profile reflected in the streetlamp only reinforced her notion that he was far more attractive than he knew.

He was hardly a sacrifice.

Nor was he arrogant at all. Part of her wanted to send a cable to Ada and Max's California hotel to remind Ada of that fact.

Before she could ruminate on that further, a slight throb at her temples had her stopping dead in her tracks. When Samuel did the same, his eyes meeting hers, she knew he felt it, too.

"There's one nearby," she said quietly, and he nodded.

"Are your stake and mallet at the ready?"

"Always," she said. "Now let's find that undead bastard."

THE GARISH, hand-painted sign outside the sprawling but rundown home declared it to be a genuine haunted house, with frequent séances held. The admission was less than Samuel would expect. Despite the gravity of the situation, he couldn't help but quickly make the conversion from pounds sterling to dollars and cents. If he believed in ghosts, he would probably consider the cost highway robbery. Twenty-five cents to see something that didn't exist was simply outrageous.

He and Violet moved quickly through the snow and crowds of people who still wandered the streets at this late hour. He patted his gloved hands against his coat pockets, reassured by the familiar feel of his stake and mallet.

His temples pounded as they approached the house, and a quick glance at Violet and the knowing look in her green eyes told him that she felt the same. There was a supernatural being in there, and for all Samuel knew there may well be a ghost, but ghosts didn't eat people. As long as he didn't have to sit at a table while some charlatan bilked the gullible of their money, ghosts could do as they please.

The next thing he did was check that he had some money on his person. There was a short queue huddled under the house's awning on the front porch, and he had to resist the impulse to push them out of the way and demand entrance. Even when vampires were nearby, the queue was sacrosanct.

Violet didn't press on ahead of the others, which he appreciated, but the vampire in the vicinity still had all of his senses on high alert. Urgency swept through him, and not for the first time he wished he could explain the situation to everyone around him so they would let them in to take care of the problem.

She tilted her face to his ear. "Part of me thinks we should offer to pay their admission so we can get in faster," she said softly. Her breath tickled his ear.

He counted at least five people ahead of them. "I don't have enough money on me for everyone," he said.

"Damn." The unladylike epithet surprised him. "I hate waiting."

But before either of them could grumble further, the small group ahead of them walked through the house's doorway, and Samuel and Violet stood before an outlandishly-dressed man wearing an old-fashioned beaver hat dyed green and a heavy black fur coat. Samuel supposed the effect was supposed to be eerie or startling, but he just looked foolish. His beard, unfashionably long and streaked with gray, only added to the effect. At least he was a human and not a vampire. Still, Samuel had to wonder if the man knew there was a vampire on the premises, or even if he was under a bloodsucker's thrall.

"Evening, sir," the man said. He nodded his head and tipped his hat at Violet. "Madam." His accent had an odd twang that Samuel couldn't place, not unlike Lambert's, but stronger.

"Good evening, sir," Samuel said, his voice as confident as he thought it would be had he ever set foot in a court of law. "Two admissions, for me and the lady."

"The missus, I expect?"

"Newlyweds," said Violet, piping up.

"My *félicitations* to you both, and that will be five cents, sir," said the man, holding out a gloved hand. The index finger was nearly worn through. Samuel removed a five-cent piece from his overcoat pocket and placed it in the man's palm.

Once the coin was stowed away in the proprietor's heavy coat and cheap paper tickets were handed over, he said, "They'll be holding a séance after midnight, if you're inclined to stick about, sir."

"I don't believe in such trifles," Samuel said. "A walk about a haunted house is sufficient."

"But I do," said Violet, smiling brightly, keeping up their ruse.

"It won't do to upset the missus so soon after the wedding," the green-hatted man said, with another tip of his head to Violet. "I'd sit in on the séance if I were you."

"I shall consider it," Samuel said, and they were finally waved through.

The house's foyer was dark, lit with flameless candles haphazardly fitted into dingy wall sconces. The carpet was wet with melting snow, its color indistinguishable in the semi-darkness. Samuel didn't care about those details, and he knew Violet wouldn't, either. There was a vampire in here, somewhere. Possibly mingling with the other people waiting to see a ghost, if the sounds of voices and nervous laughter in other rooms were anything to go by.

Hand-lettered signs, difficult to see in the dim light, instructed guests to only look in rooms whose doors were open, that divining tools were strictly forbidden without express permission from the house's medium, and that deliberately frightening other guests "by means of leaping from darkened corners" would result in being thrown out. Nothing about avoiding vampires, of course.

"Where should we start?" said Violet. She unbuttoned her coat. Almost immediately a man, shorter than the one guarding the front door but dressed in black to match, appeared from a darkened room off the foyer.

"May I take your coats?" he asked, his accent the same as the other. Samuel was itching to ask what it was but didn't dare to.

Violet shook her head. Her weapons were probably concealed in it, or her coat was at least hiding them. "No, thank you," she said.

Samuel likewise demurred. The man shrugged. "Suit yourselves, then." He pointed at a staircase, the steps covered in a grimy runner that matched the carpet. "Look upstairs if you like, the next séance starts in about twenty minutes, if you want to sit in." He wiggled his eyebrows in a way that Samuel guessed was supposed to be spooky. "Ask the spirits a question."

Samuel—and Violet undoubtedly as well—just wanted to find the bloodsucker and stake him. Or her. The question was finding out where it was hidden and stake it in a way that wouldn't draw attention from the poor sods letting themselves be fleeced in the hopes of contacting Aunt Martha from the great beyond.

He and Violet ascended the creaking staircase, following both the sounds of voices and their vampire senses. "This will have to go down as the most difficult staking in recent memory," Violet said, her voice a whisper. "There are far too many people here for our comfort. Maybe we'll get lucky and he'll be new enough to being undead and won't sense us."

"Maybe we'll get *really* lucky and there won't be any civilians to see what we're doing."

"That, too."

Of course, not having any civilians around would mean a boatload of vampires instead. There were only two of them. Samuel didn't know which would be worse.

More flameless candles sputtered from their holders as they walked up the stairs, hands in their coat pockets ready to brandish stakes and mallets. An unexpected chill had both of them shivering once they reached the landing, and Samuel's eyes met Violet's.

"Did you feel that?" she asked.

He nodded.

"Must be that spectral activity," she said. "Or a good hoax." She pointed up at the ceiling, where a grimy vent was barely visible in the semi-darkness.

Samuel didn't care. It wasn't as though ghosts were actual threats, if they existed.

The landing had two staircases leading to opposite corners of the house. Both looked to be lit up, permitted to be explored. It would be easier and quicker to split up and investigate each wing of the house separately, but it simply wasn't safe to do so. He remembered what he walked into back in the spring, that grand Mayfair home and grievously injured Adaline Sterling. Another five minutes, and she wouldn't have survived.

Just like Bert Radcliffe.

"Right or left?" Violet said. "I can't pick up which part of the house the vampire's in."

Neither could Samuel. "Right." It was the side he was closest to. If something popped out, he would be in the best position to exterminate it.

The sound of voices grew louder as they crept along the grimy carpet. Aside from the blast of frigid air at the top of the stairs, which was undoubtedly just part of the theatrics, they hadn't seen anything that might indicate the damn house was actually haunted. If he had come here and paid twenty-five cents admission expecting to see ghostly activity, he would be very put off by now.

The doors on either side of the short corridor were closed; the only light offered was that spilling from a room at the end. Samuel and Violet looked in and saw a round table set with chairs, where two women and a man, seated at it, were turned away from them. Facing them was a pale-faced, white-haired man, garbed in black like the men downstairs. A set of dogeared tarot cards rested on the tabletop in front of him.

The small group's giggles sounded mechanical and none of them turned around when the floor issued loud creaks, announcing Samuel and Violet's entrances. But the white-haired man looked up, exasperation on his face.

Oh, hell.

He quickly fixed his gaze on each of the three around the table, and their chatter and laughter abruptly ceased, like a flameless candle whose switch had been shut off. Samuel and Violet immediately readied their stakes and mallets.

The vampire's fangs extended and he stood up, jostling the table as he did so. None of the three enthralled people noticed. His eyes took on a deep red color and he hissed, vaulting himself over the table and the three people seated there at the two of them.

Oh, this was not good.

~

THE VAMPIRE CRASHED INTO SAMUEL, knocking him off-balance. Samuel quickly righted himself and pushed back, managing to get a swipe at the bloodsucker's face with the point of his stake. The vampire snarled and pushed him into the wall.

Violet withdrew a small vial of holy water from her coat pocket and splashed it at the back of the vampire's head. The smell of burning hair, then flesh, quickly assaulted her nostrils, and the vampire turned around to face her. She held out her stake and mallet. "Come over here," she said, her voice a deliberate taunt.

He advanced on her, red eyes boring into hers. Being a Searcher, descended from vampires and dhampirs herself, Violet wasn't terribly worried about being enthralled. Still, she tore her own gaze away as a safety precaution. He sprang at her, grabbing her wrist and squeezing until she dropped her holy water vial. A few drops landed on the back of his hand, and the smell of burning flesh so close to her nose made her gorge rise. The tiny glass bottle shattered on the floor. Before Violet could register what was happening, he grabbed her arm with nearly enough force to wrench it from its socket.

Hands outstretched, he froze, the expression on his face shifting to one of terror before it collapsed on itself. He quickly disintegrated, leaving nothing but a pile of oily gray ash inside his black clothing.

Samuel held up his stake and mallet triumphantly.

"Much appreciated," Violet said. "Thank you."

"The holy water was a nice touch."

"I never leave home without it." She tried to rotate her arm, and the muscle screamed in protest. That was going to hurt for a long time.

They looked at the empty clothes on the floor, then at the three people waiting for their séance, still enthralled.

"Can you break a thrall?" she asked.

He shook his head. "Too far removed down the vampire chain."

"Me, too." Left alone, they would eventually snap out of the thrall. "Can you sense any other vampires in the house? I can't."

"I think we cleared him out. Do you suppose the men downstairs know the medium was a vampire?"

"It's possible." Violet would worry about that in a few minutes. Right now, there was the matter of the vampire remains to deal with, as well as the three sitters who could fall out of their trances at any second. "What do we do about him right now?" She nudged the vampire's dusty black frock coat with her booted foot.

Samuel looked at the window. "I suggest we just dump everything out there."

It wasn't a great plan, but it was the only one they had. There wasn't a fireplace in the room, and neither of them could exactly gather everything up and walk out of the haunted house like nothing had happened.

Violet just hated to touch vampire remains. The greasy dust smelled and always left her gloves stained. "All right," she said.

The window opened on squeaky hinges, and she cringed at the noise. They couldn't spot a broom to sweep up all the ash, so they settled for shoving the clothes out the window. They could go around the house and collect them for proper disposal when they left.

Samuel shut the window with an unavoidable loud bang, and the noise seemed to startle the three people around the table back to reality.

"Where's Mr. Gregoire?" one of the women asked.

Samuel and Violet edged to the doorway. "I don't have the foggiest what you're talking about," Violet said. "We came here to sit in on a real séance and come to find there's no medium." She sighed dramatically and looked up at Samuel with what she hoped was an imploring look. "Darling, you promised me there would be ghosts."

He looked slightly taken aback at the whining tone in her voice but played along. "They must be preoccupied. Let's go, my love." He offered his ash-stained arm to her, and she looped her hand over it and they walked out of the room.

"What is this awful mess?" they heard someone exclaim behind them.

They descended the stairs, footsteps thumping the worn boards. The man who had offered to take their coats looked surprised to see them. "Everything all right? I heard a bit of a commotion upstairs."

And he hadn't come running to see that his patrons were safe. "I didn't hear a thing," Violet said. "Including ghosts. Are you certain this house is actually haunted?"

"Oh, Mr. Gregoire assures us it definitely is,"

the man said. "He's the house's owner and a real medium."

"I regret to inform you that we did not see a medium upstairs," Samuel said.

Violet held her breath, waiting for the man's reaction.

Instead of anger, he looked surprised. "There wasn't?"

"No." Samuel pinned him with a stony stare, but the man didn't flinch.

"That's odd. Mr. Gregoire must be around here somewhere."

"Have you worked for him long?"

Now the man looked a little taken aback. "No, just a couple of weeks, me and my brother. You met him. He takes the admissions. First job we were offered. Why do you ask?"

"I've worked for my share of dodgy employers," Samuel said smoothly. "I recommend that you and your brother look for work where your employer doesn't take off in the middle of the night."

They hurried away and out of the house before the man could respond. Samuel nodded to the green-hatted ticket seller, and they quickly walked into the night.

When they were a safe distance away, Violet started to giggle.

"What's so funny?" Samuel asked.

"This whole situation," she said. "It's just so ridiculous. Who goes to such an elaborate setup to enthrall people to drink their blood? It's utter madness."

"We really should investigate those brothers," Samuel said.

Her mirth faded. "How do you propose we do that?"

He exhaled, an angry sigh of frustration. His voice was an angry whisper. "I don't have the faintest clue. Damn it, why are the vampires getting more aggressive? Are they bored? Is that why they're moving into haunted houses?"

"We'll have to find Lambert and ask him," Violet said. She paused under a streetlamp, the yellow light highlighting her silver hair peeking out from under her hat. Even with the smudges of vampire ash on her coat, she still managed to look angelic. "Do you feel that?"

"Do I feel what?"

"How far removed are you from your dhampir ancestors?" Most Searchers were descended from the vampire-human hybrids; the only thing that bound them to their long-ago vampire forebears was the ability to sense and track them.

Samuel shrugged. "Great-great-great-great grandson, I believe."

"Maybe it's just me." She turned her light eyes to him. "Great times three. But I can *feel* more vampires are here, I just can't sense them nearby. Sam, *concentrate*."

He closed his eyes, trying to tune out the sounds of Niagara Falls' nightlife, the damnable cold in the air, the faint but icy winter winds. When he cleared that from his mind, he felt it. Fred Lambert's words at the hotel restaurant echoed back to him: *It's giving me a hell of a headache nearly every time the sun goes down, stronger than I've ever felt at home. Niagara Falls may very well be crawling with vampires for all I know.*

A faint vibration rang through his head, down his spine to the rest of his body, like a plucked harp string. He would have written off the sensation as an impending chill from all the travel he'd done over the last few days, but there was something … different, somehow. Like something vital inside him had been knocked off-kilter.

He focused on the vibration, and it grew a little stronger now that he noticed it.

"They're everywhere," said Violet softly. "They aren't awake, and I don't know why they wouldn't be at this time of day, and I can't count how many there are in town."

"They've been freshly turned," said Samuel. "They can't wake up yet."

"Oh, dear God," said Violet. "Samuel, we're going to have an infestation of brand new, blood-crazed vampires very soon."

Samuel opened his eyes and met hers, now wide and more than a little frightened. It pained him to see that. Truthfully, the prospect of God knew how many young vampires set him on edge, as well. He uttered a very ungentlemanly-like oath.

"Well, *fuck*."

The sun was peeking over the thinning night sky by the time they returned to their hotel. Violet and Samuel were both exhausted and frustrated. Despite the constant twang that reminded them that vampires were in the vicinity, neither of them could find their nest, nor could they track down an actual vampire to stake. Even if they had located a nest, there was a real possibility that there would be too many people about to safely execute them. Once again, Violet was stymied as to what they should do about the infestation.

Was Mr. Gregoire the one that had turned so many people and hidden them away? Violet bought a local paper before they returned to The Guild, but all she could find was information about the upcoming hot air balloon festival.

Their walk past the reception desk to the stairs did not go unnoticed. "Mr. Seecombe!" the clerk said. He sounded unnaturally chipper for someone who had to have been awake all night. He held up an envelope. "This is for you."

Samuel accepted it with a gloved hand and slipped it into his coat. "Thank you."

There were shadows under his eyes, and Violet knew there had to be matching ones under hers, too. She wanted desperately to sink into a warm bath and then sleep the day away, but she knew whatever missive was in that envelope would halt those plans. A tiny sigh escaped her. A long soak in the tub would have to wait until she returned home. She was supposed to be working.

Samuel waited until they were locked in their room before opening the envelope. Violet read the letter over his shoulder, unsurprised to see that it was from Frederick Lambert.

Mr. and Mrs. Seecombe,

I looked out for the two of you tonight and couldn't find you before I took a quick dirigible ride to St. Catharines to investigate a lead there. Found a lead and took care of it. Niagara Falls still has lots. We need more help. I took the liberty of sending a cable to New York.

I request the pleasure of your company at The Guild's tavern for luncheon today at noon. I hope that isn't too early.

F.L.

"Well, there goes our sleep," Samuel said, but he didn't sound terribly perturbed by the afternoon meeting. Neither was Violet. It had to be done. As did sending a cable to New York, which made her feel like an idiot. She should have taken care of that.

She sat down on the bed and massaged her temples. It wasn't just the vampire presence that was causing a headache this time. "Some lieutenant I am," she said.

"What do you mean?"

"What Lambert just did," she said. "We need more help here. I'm not sure how many people New York can spare, but even two or three more Searchers would be a massive help right now."

Samuel's tone was surprisingly gentle. "Violet, we've been here just over a day. Neither of us have had this kind of experience or trouble before."

"It's not just that, although I appreciate the boost of confidence. I really am a poor lieutenant. I'm better in the field." Speaking of the field, she looked down at her dress. Its hem was stained with vampire ash. "I don't suppose the hotel has a laundry service."

"Would they know how to remove rotted vampire stains?"

"Doubtful. Soap and water will have to do." She stood up, even though she wanted nothing more than to lie back and sleep. Her temples still faintly ached, as did her arm from where the vampire tried to rip it from her shoulder. "I need some sleep before we meet with Lambert, and I have to clean this dress as much as I can. I didn't bring enough clothing with me to let it go until I return home." She tried to reach for her skirt's fastenings at her back and winced in pain. Her injured arm wasn't cooperating. "I'll also need some help getting undressed."

Samuel had the grace to blush at the prospect.

"I'll heal fast enough, but that vampire really hurt my arm. I can't lift it."

"No," he said quickly. "I don't mind."

"The pins in my hair, too."

He started with the pins, gently plucking each one from her hair and lining them up on top of the chest of drawers. When her thick mass of silver hair finally fell free, she let out a little sigh of relief.

As if he could read her mind, he massaged his fingers against her scalp. Had she the ability, she would have purred. "Thank you," she said.

"Do you need help brushing it out?"

She didn't know which surprised her more: the offer, or the unexpected husky note in his voice. A shiver went down her spine, one she hoped he hadn't noticed in case she was off about his voice. Maybe he was just tired. God knew she was.

"Please." She surprised herself when she heard the breathy quality that leached into her voice. Oops.

He picked up her brush and gave her hair a few long strokes. When he stepped away, she reached for the buttons on her blouse, knowing she wouldn't be able to ease it off her shoulders without help. Not wanting to make this situation any more awkward than it needed to be, she made short work of the buttons and noticed that Samuel averted his gaze when he slid the garment off her shoulders. He unbuttoned her skirt and she stepped out of it, trying not sigh again at the stains the vampire's ash left at the hem.

"I'm going to need some help with my nightdress," she said. Samuel, bless him, looked around their shared room, anywhere but at her. "I'd do the same for you," she said. "Help you get undressed for bed."

"I have no doubt that you would."

"You aren't used to working with women."

"No, although it doesn't bother me."

She rotated her shoulder again. At least nothing was broken, although it was going to be sore for quite some time. "Would it be easier I turned down the light?" she asked. She moved to the oil lamp and turned down the flame before he could answer.

"It's not a problem." He still kept his eyes averted as she shed her corset and stockings as quickly as she could.

Samuel moved through the near-darkness, her nightdress in hand. It took some maneuvering to get her injured arm through its long sleeves, made more difficult by his looking away. *For God's sake.* Field injuries happened. Just because he wasn't used to working with women didn't mean he couldn't get past this hang-up. "You're making this difficult."

"I'm not trying to."

"I know, but you are. Just… just look at my face if it'll help you. You're acting like you've never seen someone in the altogether before."

That remark drew something that sounded like a muffled laugh from him, and Violet supposed that was the closest thing she was going to get that resembled amusement from him.

"Not quite in this situation," he finally said. His eyes fixed on hers, and even in the darkness Violet could see the intensity reflected there.

All right, she knew he would have noticed *that* shiver coming from her. Well, there wasn't any point in being embarrassed about that.

Her nightdress over her head, she finally sat down on the edge of the bed, ready for a few hours' worth of sleep. "If it makes you feel better, I can help you undress," she said.

He turned away from her, and Violet averted her eyes. "I can manage on my own, but thank you for the offer." There was a rustle of fabric as he started shucking his clothes. Violet let her mind wander—what did he look like? Where had he been scarred by vampires?

"Another time, maybe?" She didn't bother to try hiding the teasing note in her voice. Why not?

The rustling paused for a few seconds, and he didn't reply for a long minute. Violet thought she might have angered or offended him, and she held her breath, waiting.

His voice was calm, neutral, when he did. "Perhaps."

~

It was only slightly less tortuous helping Violet get dressed than it was helping her get ready for bed.

Damn it, Samuel was not good at this.

Her being a good Searcher wasn't the issue. His completely inappropriate attraction to her was. She was a lovely woman, and intelligent, and she even managed to have a sense of humor about this whole strange situation. She was so unlike what he was used to back home, and it wasn't just working with her.

He'd turned away from her as soon as he could before she had a chance to notice just how helping her affected him. Once away from her gaze, tried to will his erection away before he joined her in bed. Nothing he thought about had worked; all he could think about was Violet's shining hair and smooth skin the dim light of the oil lamp revealed.

He'd gone to bed stiff and uncomfortable, and hadn't slept well.

Violet, of course, was wide awake and ready to see Lambert when they woke up later that morning. She pronounced her arm and shoulder as feeling much better and only needed a little help getting dressed, asking Samuel to help her with her blouse and putting a couple of pins in her hair.

Lambert was waiting when they made their way to the hotel's restaurant, standing when he saw

Violet approach. Samuel pulled out her chair for her, and all three of them sat down.

Lambert's expression was grim. "How did last night go?" he asked.

Violet kept her voice low. "We found one in a haunted house attraction. He was pretending to hold séances and enthralling the people who sat in. There were a couple of other people helping with the attraction, but we don't know if they knew their employer was a vampire." She told Lambert about the brothers, and their story about the strange owner of the house.

"How was your hunting last night?" Samuel asked Lambert.

"Two staked," Lambert said. "More to go. I've wired for help from Toronto and Montreal, but no one can spare anyone else right now."

"I'm sure New York will be able to send someone," Violet said. "At least I hope so."

"We're all short on hunters," Lambert said. Frustration tinged his voice. "I think we should return to that haunted house today and see if we can't find more vampires there." Disapproval tugged the corners of his mouth downward. "Why didn't you stay and investigate further last night?"

"There were too many people," Samuel said. "It simply wasn't possible, and those brothers watching the house wouldn't have let us poke around. Miss Singer injured her arm, as well."

Concern flashed across Lambert's face. "What happened?"

Violet half-shrugged with her good shoulder. "It wasn't that bad. The vampire we staked managed to get a good grip on me, is all. I'm already on the mend. But going back to Samuel's point, it wasn't practical or safe to do so, and if there's a nest of the size we're all sensing, it wouldn't have been a fair fight anyway."

Lambert looked somewhat mollified at this statement. "Of course."

"It makes more sense to look while they're sleeping," Violet said. "Fred, maybe you've had better luck than I have. Have you noticed any more missing persons reports? There don't seem to be an unusual number in Niagara Falls, but all the papers keep printing is fluff about the weather and that hot air balloon show."

"The Toronto branch sent a cable last night," he replied. "They've been monitoring missing persons reports, and there's been a spike in recent months across southern Ontario and the northern states. The only thing these people have in common is that they were reasonably young and traveling alone at night, and never made it to their destinations."

Violet and Samuel nodded. Vampires preferred to turn younger adults rather than children or older people. It was part of their *modus operandi*; it was easier to prey on unsuspecting and weaker beings when one was young and beautiful.

"And none of the local law enforcement have noticed patterns?" Samuel asked.

Lambert shook his head. "Not to our knowledge. It isn't terribly difficult to not be found if you know how to cover your tracks, and it isn't uncommon for someone to vanish when they're traveling alone, especially in rural areas at night." He leaned back in his seat and regarded Samuel coolly. "They don't warn you not to wander around in the middle of the night back in jolly old England?"

"Of course we do," Samuel said, ignoring the

slight. "England doesn't have nearly as much backcountry as you do here."

"Point taken."

Violet's eyes darted between the two of them, irritation across her face at the exchange. Truthfully, Samuel didn't know why he and Lambert interacted with such a thin veneer of civility between them, either.

You do, and the reason is sitting next to you. And he *doesn't want you on his territory, either.*

Samuel couldn't figure that one out. Frederick Lambert didn't seem to have a problem with Violet working on this case. He was the one who had asked for New York's help, after all.

Perhaps he was imagining issues where there were none, or that he'd created himself. He didn't have any claim on Violet.

They finished their meal in silence and walked out of the hotel to the cold, snowy streets. The sun made it almost tolerable, but Samuel still kept his gloved hands in his pockets.

The haunted house was closed up for the day, its signs taken down. It looked like an ordinary, albeit dilapidated, old house, and when Lambert knocked on the door, no one answered. He waited a few moments and tried again.

"Maybe there's a door around the back?" he said. "I don't know about you two, but..." He tapped his temple. Samuel and Violet nodded. It was faint but constant. There was a vampire nest nearby, if not in the house itself.

Footprints already marred the snow around the house, alleviating worries of leaving tracks. Still, they were careful to look around the street, now fairly quiet this time of day, and quickly slipped around the porch without anyone questioning them.

Another door led into the house, and on the far side of the house, a pair of black-painted cellar doors beckoned, more footprints leading to it. "I feel like this might be too simple," Violet said. A heavy padlock was looped around the doors' handles.

Samuel removed a lock-picking kit from his pocket, to Violet's and Lambert's obvious approval. He made quick work of the lock and quickly popped it off, leaving it in the snow. He lifted one of the doors and peered in the darkened cellar.

The smell of something rotting had all three of them gasping for the cold air. Violet reached for an embroidered handkerchief and held it over her mouth.

"Oh, my God," said Lambert. "What the bloody hell were they *eating*?"

He and Samuel swung open the doors to let the sunlight in, then descended the short, rickety staircase to the cellar, Violet trailing behind. Already they could smell something rotten starting to cook. The body sprawled haphazardly across the dirt floor, its skin already splitting and peeling in the sunlight, confirmed what they already knew.

Samuel cursed himself for not bringing a lantern or even a flameless candle, but it wasn't as though three people could carry lanterns in the middle of the afternoon, on the street, without being noticed. It was already risky walking into the cellar and leaving the doors wide open for anyone to see. They would have to work quickly.

As his eyes adjusted to the darkness, he counted eleven vampires in the cellar. They split up in the small space, breathing shallowly, as they staked each of the sleeping vampires. The source of the foul stench was, unfortunately, found in Samuel's section of the cellar, in the form of dead raccoons. The animals had been ripped apart, undoubtedly in the red haze of bloodlust common to new vampires. Pain squeezed Samuel's heart, briefly. The poor beasts didn't deserve to die like that, no one did.

Including people, if that's what they were doing. And Samuel had his concerns about that. Why weren't there more missing people here, if a new vampire army was being assembled?

And new vampires they were. All of them took longer to disintegrate and their bodies were more resistant to stakes than the older ones they were used to dealing with. That only added to the odor permeating through the cellar. Samuel thought he might actually be sick. It was so much like stabbing a real, sleeping person when they'd been turned so recently. It was harder to remember that they were monsters.

Violet was the first to head back to the stairs. "How is everyone's head doing?" she asked. "My headache's starting to ease a little."

"Mine, too," said Lambert. He sounded unwell. Samuel couldn't blame him.

"As is mine." That didn't mean their trip to Niagara Falls was complete. If they couldn't sense the vampire who turned the ones littering the dirt floor, that could mean he or she was still out there. Master vampires wouldn't leave a nest of fledglings on their own. It took time for them to learn to control their bloodlust, how to be a proper vampire.

Well, at least those who *wanted* to learn how to be a proper vampire. Samuel had dealt with plenty who couldn't have the decency to slink around the shadows.

And not eat people? If all they did was eat the local wildlife, there wouldn't be any need for the Searchers.

His gaze happened upon the pile of mangled raccoon remains, and his stomach lurched in response. *Perhaps not.*

Lambert was the first person out of the cellar, and he turned away from Samuel and Violet, noisily vomiting into the snow. Violet's eyes locked with Samuel's, a glassy shine to them.

"I feel like doing the same," she said, her voice queasy.

Samuel closed the cellar doors and fastened the padlock over the handles. "Will you be sick?"

She closed her eyes and breathed deeply. "No, I think I'll be all right." She tilted her head in Lambert's direction. "Fred? What about you?"

Lambert straightened and adjusted his hat. His face was pale and a fine sheen of sweat streaked down his face. His voice was a harsh rasp. "I'm not dead yet. What the hell was down there?"

"It appears they've been eating the local fauna," Samuel said. "Which explains why there aren't more missing people in Niagara Falls."

"And their maker isn't in there, unless the one we staked last night was their maker," Violet added.

"That's possible." It would make sense,

"But we don't know for certain. I don't think anyone should be resting easy until we've staked a few more," said Lambert. He took a shaky breath, and for half a second Samuel thought he might be sick again. He looked back at the now-locked cellar doors. "We should get out of here before anyone notices us."

They walked through the snow back to the front of the house, but their hopes for not being noticed were quickly dashed when a familiar voice said, "What the hell are you doing here?"

All three of them looked at the porch, where the pair of brothers from the night before stood. The front door was still closed and no one had heard it open, so Samuel guessed that they didn't live here, either.

"Nothing," said Lambert.

One of them peered at Samuel and Violet before recognition bloomed across his face. "You were here last night!" he said. "I remember her hair!"

"I shall have to find a better hat," Violet said, her voice nearly a grumble.

"Are you looking for Gregoire, too?" the man asked. Both he and his brother seemed a little less suspicious of them.

"No," said Samuel smoothly, quickly coming up with a lie. "I told you last night that my wife is very interested in matters of the paranormal and spiritualism. She wanted to see if she could sense any ghosts here in the daytime."

"You must really love her. It's fuckin' freezing out here," the other brother said. He tilted his head toward Violet. "Begging your pardon, madam."

Violet nodded regally in return.

"Well, we haven't found any evidence of ghosts," said Samuel. "Just like we didn't last night, either."

"I was very disappointed," said Violet, playing along.

"Yeah, well, to tell the truth, I think Gregoire's full of shit," said the older brother.

"All mediums are," said the other, disgust curling his upper lip.

Samuel exchanged glances with Violet and Lambert. It was looking more and more like these two didn't know what their former employer was. "My wife doesn't share your views," he said. "I suppose neither of you have witnessed spirits in your house?"

"It's not ours," said the oldest. "We're renting rooms at a boarding house about half a mile away. Thinking about trying our luck in America next."

"I'd rather go back to Halifax," said the other.

"So you've never seen ghosts in there?" Violet asked, disappointment in her voice. She was piling it on a little too thick, in Samuel's estimation, although the brothers seemed to fall for it.

"No," said the older one. "Though I don't believe in 'em, anyway."

"Gregoire was plenty strange without ghosts," said the other. "I'm Chester, by the way. Chester Graves. This here's Morris." He pointed a thumb at his older brother.

"If you're looking for places to go, I'd recommend going back to Halifax," Lambert said.

"There's nothing for us there," said Morris. "I'm thinking we should go on to New York or Chicago next. Get some work at one of the airfield sites."

Airfield construction was dirty and dangerous work, but Samuel could see the appeal. It was supposed to pay well, not that he'd ever worked on one.

Samuel wanted to ask if they'd ever been in the cellar, but he couldn't fathom a way to do so in a roundabout way that wouldn't tell the Graves brothers what they discovered down there. Instead, he said, "I'm sure working on an airfield will be less strange than for a medium."

"Mediums pay rather good," Chester said. "Even if they're weird. 'Don't go in this room, don't go in that room, stay at the front of the house.' He was loony."

"Took off last night and didn't pay us," Morris said.

"Perhaps it's best that you leave Niagara Falls," said Violet. "We may not have seen any ghosts last night or today, but I still have a strange feeling about your employer. You should leave."

NIGHT FELL EARLY, and she and Samuel left their hotel shortly after sunset. This time, Violet could pick up the faint vibration that said vampires were nearby, but she couldn't pinpoint an exact location. She looked up at Samuel under the light from the street lamps, and could tell that he felt it, too. There was another nest somewhere close by, if not more, but she couldn't pinpoint it. It was a low thrum, a never-ending vibration that alerted them to their presence.

They couldn't sit around their hotel room and wait for one of them to show up, so they did what they had to every night: hunt. And, Violet thought wryly, take in some of Niagara Falls's life after dark. She didn't often get an opportunity to travel, even if it was only a few hours away from home.

She could tell Samuel was cagey as they walked along the snowy streets, and she was, too. This was new territory for both of them; not just because neither was familiar with the infested town but being thrown together with a very different partner. Well, not exactly thrown together. She had volunteered, after all. So had Samuel.

"Why didn't you go right back to London after Ada and Max's wedding?" she asked. "You were so eager to come to Canada right away."

He seemed surprised by the question and took a few seconds to answer. "I suppose I needed a change of scenery."

"You've said that, but why?" She prodded a little further. "What happened back in London? Was it Ada's accident?"

Accident. That was a hell of a way to describe nearly having one's throat ripped out.

"No, not exactly." Samuel continued walking. "It happened after the incident with Mrs. Sterling, last autumn."

Violet forced herself to keep from urging him on and waited.

"I don't enjoy discussing the particulars of it," he said. "But…"

"Sometimes it helps to talk about things with someone who's experienced them as well," she said gently.

"It was a routine vampire hunt," he said, his voice abrupt. "One of my partners died."

Violet assumed as much, but she merely nodded. "I'm sorry."

"He was a new Searcher. Bert Radcliffe. Just a lad, only nineteen. He overestimated his own ability with the stake and underestimated the vampire's strength. He bled out in front of me."

When Violet looked at his face, she saw his eyes had taken on a glazed look, like he was back in the cellar or drawing room or wherever that vampire had killed his partner. Nineteen years old. A hell of a way to die.

"I've seen it happen before," Samuel said. "But not in someone so young, and not on their first hunt. He was young, dumb, and arrogant. Just like I was at nineteen." He looked straight ahead, at the steam cab that a small group of women were pouring into. "I stopped hunting after Radcliffe was killed. I wasn't ready to do it again until I came to New York."

"I couldn't tell," she said, thinking of the way he dispatched Gregoire the night prior.

"We'll see how I perform when faced with more than one vampire. I don't have as much confidence in my skills as I used to." He barked out a short, humorless laugh. "That's a hell of a thing for you to deal with, too. Your partner dropped the basket."

Violet knew that trying to soothe his ego would probably be fruitless, but she had to try anyway. "Sam, that's one of the risks of our profession…"

He cut her off. "It's never happened to me before," he said. His eyes blazed when they met hers, but she still saw the agony and guilt reflected there under the street lamp. "He shouldn't have been in the field yet, but we were desperate for more help. He said he was ready, and…"

"He wasn't," Violet said, finishing for him. "All nineteen-year-olds think they're ready. It's part of being that age."

"How old was Mrs. Sterling when she conducted her first hunt?"

He had her there. "About seventeen, same age I was when I started. But we'd been practicing for years. Samuel, how strong was this boy's sense?"

It was the wrong question to ask. He visibly

stiffened at her words, his mouth tugging downward. "Not like mine. I'm not sure how far removed he was from his dhampir ancestors."

An inexperienced boy, without as much as the sense as other Searchers, working for a branch that was dangerously understaffed—it was a recipe for catastrophe. A bubble of grief welled up in Violet at the thought of the boy being struck down so young. Then she remembered the pair of brothers who'd turned up on Goat Island, and all the young vampires they'd staked with Lambert earlier in the day.

Samuel bent down and whispered in her ear, breath tickling the delicate skin there. The sensation jarred her out of her thoughts. "Bat."

"Beg your pardon?"

"Bat," he said, and discreetly pointed a gloved finger at a shop that advertised small automatons in its window. "It just landed on that roof."

The increase in pressure to her temples has been so slight that Violet hadn't noticed it until now.

"There's only one reason a bat would be flying about in January in Canada," she said.

"Do you have your stake at the ready?"

"Always." She smiled at him, and he thawed a few degrees. "Let's go."

IT FELT like they had been wandering around Niagara Falls's snowy streets for hours, but when Violet checked the watch she kept in her pocket, she saw only forty-five minutes had passed. That stupid bat had flitted from building to building, to the tops of street lamps, and even threatened to crash into the heads of unsuspecting people a few times. Whether it knew it was being followed, Violet couldn't say, but it was certainly either very bold, very stupid, or both.

Violet was betting on stupid. She was *hoping* for stupid. She didn't feel like having a fight with a vampire tonight. While she was able to keep up with Samuel, the cold and exhaustion from lack of sleep still pulled at her.

The bat darted past them and landed on a street lamp. Its yellow light illuminated an icy, steep walkway that led to a small dock. "Damn," said Violet. She was appropriately dressed for the weather, but navigating that incline would be treacherous.

Samuel gripped her arm reassuringly, but whether the gesture was for her or himself, she couldn't tell. "It's moving forward," he said, voice low in her ear. A shiver that had nothing to do with the cold ribboned through her. "What the devil is that boat doing in January?"

"It's a Niagara Falls sightseeing boat," she replied. "The *Maid of the Mist*. I rode it when I was a little girl."

Samuel kept propelling both of them forward down the icy incline. "I think our friend intends to board it," he said.

"Damn," she said again. "What the hell does a vampire want on a tour boat?"

The bat swooped to the covered deck of the boat. They hurried to reach the gate, Samuel already reaching for his coat pocket. "Two, please," he said to the unsuspecting ticket taker. "Are we too late?"

The man stared at him before speaking. "Yes,

sir. The *Maid of the Mist* is standing room only at night in January."

Violet loathed sarcasm.

Samuel opened his mouth to offer a rebuttal, but Violet spoke first. She clutched his arm a little more tightly. "Darling, just pay him," she said. To the ticket taker, she said, "We really aren't too late, are we?"

He softened a little. "Boat departs in five minutes. Be sure to pick up a blanket and stay inside. It's bloody cold out there."

Violet was not looking forward to that, and judging from the set line of Samuel's mouth, he wasn't, either. But he paid for another tourist attraction that was going to end up a greasy mess for them.

For *them*, she reminded herself. That vampire didn't have a chance.

The enclosed lounge on the deck was almost humid with its steam-powered heaters, but after the cold of the outdoors Violet welcomed it. Still, she draped one of the fur blankets piled beside the deck door around her shoulders, trying to coax some more warmth into her body. It might come in use if she had to trap the vampire with it.

And that undead flying bastard was on the boat somewhere, she could *feel* it.

The boat's engines roared to life, hot steam issuing from every vent onboard. It lurched forward, and Violet nearly crashed into Samuel as it started moving.

"Steady," he said. "We have to find that thing."

She nodded and looked around the lounge. There were perhaps ten passengers willing to brave the cold and damp to see what they could of the waterfalls at night. *Utter lunatics.*

As was the vampire: the lunatic, utterly stupid vampire who shifted into a bat and would shortly be dealing with freezing cold water from the never-ending flow of the falls. Although she had to admit that the vampire wouldn't care about the cold, assuming he even noticed it.

The vampire certainly wasn't in the lounge, which was a mixed blessing. It would hopefully reduce the risk of the other passengers seeing it staked, but they would have to go out into the bone-chilling cold to do so. Violet already missed the warmth of the lounge and they hadn't even left yet.

She and Samuel avoided eye contact with everyone else and slipped out the flimsy lounge door to the deck. Violet bit back a gasp of shock as the freezing air and droplets flung from the falls stabbed her face with what felt like a thousand tiny, icy needles, and judging from the horrified look on Samuel's face, he felt it, too. It was almost difficult to differentiate this new type of pain from the one that still permeated through her head.

And the *noise*. The roar of the rushing water was nearly deafening, and she had to strain to hear Samuel's order to move to the back of the boat.

Forcing herself to breathe the frigid air, they walked along the slippery deck to the stern. The light offered by the lanterns strung along the deck was hardly sufficient, but it still shone brightly enough to reveal a very pale, very naked man, thankfully alone, looking up at the falls in abject shock. He didn't notice Samuel and Violet approaching him until they were only a few feet away, stakes and mallets in hand.

Despite the cold, Violet shrugged off the heavy fur blanket wrapped around her shoulders, needing to have as much mobility as possible. She and Samuel both stood with their feet shoulder-length apart, trying to keep their purchase on the iced-over deck.

This is madness.

Neither she nor Samuel wore life vests. If the vampire was inclined to, he could toss them over the edge of the boat and no one would know until their bodies washed up ashore. *If* they washed up. God knew how many poor souls had ended up sucked into the Niagara Gorge never to be seen again, their flesh stripped away by the never-ending churn of the water.

They hadn't thought things through. They should have looked for life vests first… the boat's railing was so close … all it would take was one errant wave to tilt it to the side and sweep them away…

"I can't feel it!" the vampire screamed. He turned wild eyes to Samuel and Violet. *"I can't feel the fucking cold!"*

The panicked look on his face was replaced by something resembling hunger, and Violet could see his eyes shift red with bloodlust as he realized what was in front of him. Two meals, neither of whom had their sea legs in the middle of a freezing river. "This almost makes up for it," he said. He advanced on them, bare feet gliding over the deck. He stumbled as he advanced on Violet, and Samuel took that opportunity to knock him to the deck. Violet threw her blanket over him for added measure.

There was a brief struggle as he tried to free himself from the blanket, but neither of them let go. Samuel fumbled with his stake, placing it over what was probably the vampire's torso, but before he could deliver the fatal strike, the vampire gave a guttural hiss and pushed them off him.

Violet was flung against the side of the boat, the impact knocking the wind out of her. She saw Samuel rise to his feet, albeit unsteadily. When she tried to do the same, she slipped back to the deck, smacking her elbow in the process. Pain zigzagged through her arm, then numbness. She briefly prayed that she hadn't broken it.

The sound of wet feet slapping against the deck managed to override even the roar of the falls, the base of which the boat was rapidly approaching. Violet tried to scramble to her feet but slid back to the deck again.

The vampire placed his hands on her shoulders, pinning her in place. His fingers dug into her through her coat, and he leaned his face down to hers. His breath stank of decayed flesh, and a wave of nausea rolled over Violet.

Perhaps that's simply the waves.

He opened his mouth, fangs extended, and yanked her head to the side, exposing as much of her neck as he could. Her hat rolled off her head, but she scarcely noticed the cold and frozen droplets whistling through her ears and hair.

This is it. I'm going to be eaten on a boat in the dead of winter.

But surprise suffused the vampire's face as he was shoved aside, back to the deck. Violet scrabbled to her feet and picked up the stake and mallet that had been knocked from her hands, delivering a vicious kick to the monster's leg when he tried to stand up again. The ice coating the deck finally seemed to have bested him, and he couldn't rise to his feet again.

Without another second of hesitation, Samuel

leaped on to the vampire and delivered a well-placed stake to the creature's heart.

Time seemed to have stopped for an eternity as they waited for the vampire to crumble into dust. It wasn't until he started to disintegrate that Violet realized her own heart was still pounding and her palms were sweaty inside her gloves. Pure terror still coursed through her, even though the pain in her temples had finally ceased. The vampire was disposed of.

She nearly hadn't made it. When was the last time she'd had such a close call?

Samuel grabbed her in a hug, his breath raspy in her ear. "Good God," he said. "I nearly lost you."

She didn't try to argue with him. Had Samuel not been there, had he not jumped in when he did, she wouldn't have made it off the boat. "Th-thank you," she said, teeth chattering in the cold and in her fright. "I'm sorry. I didn't mean to botch that. I…"

"It's all right," he said. "He's dead. That's the important thing."

"The hell's going on here?"

They couldn't see the interloper, probably one of the boat's crew, but they would soon. And they would probably have to have a good reason for being on the deck at this time of night, which they didn't have.

What are they going to do? Toss us overboard?

There was still the matter of the greasy stain that had been the vampire that was still on the deck. It wasn't bright enough to see clearly, but she was willing to wager that whoever was looking for them would have a lantern at least, if not a flameless one that offered better light. *Damn it!*

Samuel seemed to realize their dilemma at the same time. He quickly stepped over the stain and wrapped his arms around Violet's waist, bringing her closer to him.

"Who's out here? Are you crazy?" There was that voice again, and closer. Violet heard a muffled curse and a thump. He must have stumbled on the deck. Her whole body still hurt from sliding around.

Samuel slanted his mouth over hers just as the bright light of a flameless lantern was flashed in their faces. Violet gasped from surprise but didn't pull away. Instead, she found her arms reaching around his neck and she kissed him back, forgetting for a few seconds that they were standing over a vampire's remains, on a freezing boat at the base of Niagara Falls.

It would have been romantic, had it not been to maintain their cover, or hide those remains. Or if it hadn't been the dead of winter.

The sound of a throat being cleared and light splashing across their eyes had them pulling apart. "You know how dangerous it is to be out here without a life vest?" The man wore a heavy fur coat, not unlike the ones the Graves brothers wore at the haunted house the night before, and a life vest over it.

"We, um…" Violet fumbled for words. How the hell could a kiss from Samuel Seecombe of all people leave her weak-kneed and speechless?

She sneaked a glance at him. Well, the man had just saved her life. Twice. And he wasn't bad-looking to boot, either.

But he *was* her colleague.

"My wife wished for some fresh air," Samuel said briskly, rising to his full height.

"Your wife," said the man. "Wanted some air."

He clearly didn't believe them, but Violet knew he wasn't in a position to argue with them. What had they done wrong, aside from wander from the covered, poorly heated lounge at the bow?

"Yes," said Samuel. He pressed his hand into the small of Violet's back. "And now that we've had some, we are returning to the lounge."

"Make it quick," the man said. "We're turning back in a few minutes." He waited until they walked ahead of him and held up his lantern to light the way.

"Crazy Brits," he said, as they walked into the lounge.

"Crazy American," Violet said softly. Samuel's mouth quirked up at the corners.

The heat, as patchy as it was, was welcome to Violet, and she took a seat on a scarred wooden bench. Samuel sat down beside her, and Violet felt a little self-conscious. What on earth had possessed him to…

Don't think about it too much, she chided herself. *It's been ages since a man's taken interest in you, even if it was just to cover up a dead vampire.*

As if echoing her thoughts, Samuel said, "I apologize."

"Don't," she said.

"But I—"

"Sam, I'm not angry," she said. "Nor am I going to fall to the deck in a fit of vapors."

"You don't seem the vapors type."

"Nor hysterical," she said. "You've saved my life twice these last few days."

"He nearly got you," Samuel said, his voice soft and desolate. The regret there tore at Violet's heart, and she wrapped his hands in her own, trying to be as reassuring as she could. "I nearly had him, and I don't think either of us are used to working under these conditions. If I hadn't—"

"But you did. And I'm fine." Her elbow throbbed, but the feeling had returned to it. She was going to have some terrible bruising over the next few days, but that was better than having a broken limb amputated, or viscera ripped from her body. She thought of Ada Sterling's ordeal in London and shuddered.

The boat's engines groaned under their feet, and through the lounge's portholes she could see the bright lights of the town on the shore. There were a few shouts as workers docked the boat, and around them, the other passengers started to rise and shed the heavy blankets the *Maid of the Mist* provided.

Samuel helped Violet to her feet, taking care with her injured elbow. "Sam?" she said.

"Yes?"

"Don't apologize for kissing me," she said. "Ever."

FIVE

Samuel didn't let go of Violet's arm until they were back on the cold street, terrified that if he released her, something else would slither out of a dark corner and try to hurt her again. His mind still reeled from what had happened on the boat; the images of Violet falling to the slippery deck, unable to defend herself against that vampire continuing to flash before his eyes.

His reaction reminded him of what happened to him after Radcliffe died. Even when he looked at Violet, he couldn't keep his heart from pounding so hard against his ribs that he thought she could hear it. He couldn't keep himself from doing it, just to make doubly sure she was still there.

And these types of incidents happened all the time during vampire hunts. It was why they preferred to work in pairs or groups. Samuel had been saved by his partners before and he'd saved others. Bert Radcliffe wasn't the first Searcher to die in front of him, but he had been the youngest and most inexperienced. Samuel had hated the helpless feeling that overcame him every time he saw someone in danger, even though he'd still been able to do his job.

He loathed feeling insecure.

Then there was that kiss, which only made everything more muddled. She wasn't angry about it and even seemed encouraging toward him doing it again, but it was so out of character for him that he wasn't sure he could.

He liked and respected Violet very much. More than that, he had to admit. Which made him a very bad partner. Distractions could prove fatal in this business.

Best to keep it hidden away, like he did his grief over Radcliffe's death. Violet had chipped away at that part of himself he kept hidden from the rest of the world, and he was conflicted about that. He didn't want to admit that weakness or his failure, but it felt good to get it off his chest, if only a little, to have Violet's sympathetic ear and know she didn't hate or judge him for what happened to poor Radcliffe.

Samuel did. He held himself and the entire London branch responsible for what happened to the boy. Radcliffe hadn't been ready, but the branch had been desperate for more Searchers and brushed aside any question of him not being prepared.

The London Searchers needed more than new hunters. Like Ada Sterling had said so many months ago, everything about the way that branch functioned needed to be changed.

He forced himself out of his thoughts and returned them to the woman he still held on to. "We should return to the hotel and see about your arm."

"It'll be fine," she said.

"You said that about the injury Gregoire left you with."

"And I was fine." She gave him a look that brooked no argument. "And I'm fine now, too."

Samuel didn't press her further and instead changed the subject. "Are you sensing anything nearby?"

She shook her head. "Not yet, but the night is still young. Lambert said there must be more vampires in the area. I believe him."

Violet was right. There were still many hours left until sunrise, and it would be irresponsible of them to return to the hotel when she insisted she was fine. He had the impression that if she wasn't, she would tell him. Hunting with an injured partner could be just as dangerous as hunting alone.

"Do you want some roasted chestnuts?" she asked.

Roasted chestnuts? How could she think of food at a time like this? He shot her a look that he knew had to be incredulous, but she merely smiled, her sore arm and the *Maid of the Mist* apparently pushed aside.

For now.

Why the hell not?

"Why not?" he said, echoing his thoughts.

She smiled, and his heart unexpectedly fluttered. He couldn't remember the last time that happened, and he knew it was all because of Violet and her quip as they left the boat. *Don't ever apologize for kissing me.*

It had been impulsive, the only thing he could think to do to hide from the boat's workers what they'd killed on the deck. And it was for himself, as well. For a few horrifying seconds he'd thought he was going to watch someone else be killed, and the relief that had poured through him had been unlike anything else he'd felt. He needed to make sure she was still there, whole and alive.

For the first time in his life, he came close to understanding what Maximilian Sterling had felt when he saw that vampire in London rip into Ada's neck.

Violet bought some chestnuts from a street vendor before he could offer to pay for them and they kept on walking along the street. A comfortable silence descended over them as they stepped over ice, until Samuel finally had to speak about one of the things plaguing him since they arrived in Niagara Falls. "I'm not at my best right now," he said.

"I know." She spoke matter-of-factly, without a trace of anger or frustration in her voice. "And I don't want you to torment yourself over it. Sooner or later Searchers have to go back into the field. We've faced two vampires since we arrived and destroyed both."

"And the cellar."

"Does the cellar really count, though? They were sleeping." She ate a chestnut before speaking again. "You still know what to do. Your reflexes and training are still there. 'Muscle memory,' I think it's called."

She was too understanding. It would have irritated him, if he didn't want more of it. When was the last time he messed up something and hadn't had horrible consequences afterward? A memory of his father, also a Searcher, pushing him into a closet and locking him in for some unimportant slight when he was twelve popped up unbidden into his mind. He pushed it away impatiently.

Violet continued. "Besides all of that, we'll have some help soon. I sent a cable to New York. No one will ignore the orders of the Searcher lieutenant."

A role she didn't want, he remembered. "What will the New York branch do when you resign?"

"You sound as if I'm definitely going to resign."

"Why not? You've said you don't want it."

She shrugged. "Hold an election, if necessary, but I have someone else in mind who I think would be a good fit. The Singers have been running the branch for years and it's time someone else did it."

"You advocate a democracy, then."

"Yes." She looked away for a moment, her expression unreadable. "Until my Uncle Angus took over the branch, my family ran it in a well—problematic way, I suppose. The ends always justified the means, no matter who was hurt."

"Much the same way London still runs theirs."

"Precisely."

"Were your parents Searchers?"

"Yes, although they've both passed on now. My mother died when I was a baby. My father was the branch head but died of consumption when I was twenty. I inherited his flat." She looked down at her half-finished box of chestnuts. "Family money, made in alchemy schemes long before he was born. You know there isn't a great deal to be made in hunting vampires."

He did, coming from family money himself.

She gave a short, frustrated sigh. "There was plenty to be made in alchemy in my great-great-great-grandfather's time." Her expression grew serious again. "At least until he met my vampire great-great-great-grandmother and they created my dhampir ancestors. Anyway, my father was unwilling to offer better compensation to other Searchers. He manipulated people with the sense into continuing to work for him using moral arguments. You can't survive on morals or good intentions."

"And you and your uncle have tried to improve wages?"

She nodded. "We have our homes, passed down through generations, but that's it. I'm not a particularly wealthy woman, but I have enough and I'm willing to share."

It was more than his colleagues in London were willing to do. At least Violet and Angus Singer understood that change needed to occur and were making strides toward it.

"That was quick thinking back on the boat," she said, changing the subject.

He knew immediately what she referred to, and he felt himself blush like a lovestruck lad. He was grateful for the low light offered by the street lamps.

"Ah, well," he said, his voice a low mumble. "I told you I'm sorry about that."

"And I told you no apology was necessary. Look, Sam, I like and respect you. You've saved me twice since we met."

Why did she want to talk about this? Not that Samuel didn't find her intelligent or charming or attractive, because he did, but because he couldn't say the same about himself anymore. Despite her kind words, he wasn't the cocksure bastard he'd been before, that Ada Sterling had undoubtedly told her all about. He hated feeling weak and unsure.

Six months ago, he would've done more than

kiss her if given the opportunity. He wouldn't have apologized for doing it, either.

Samuel had completely lost sight of who he was, and Violet didn't seem to understand that. He didn't know how to respond to her, or anyone, anymore.

He realized belatedly that she was waiting for a response. "I like and respect you as well," he said, his voice stiff. The words he would have used before Radcliffe's death escaped him; all he could remember in that moment was that they would probably be crude and lascivious.

He may as well be honest. "Violet, I'm not who I used to be," he said.

"I know. You've told me yourself several times. And Ada and Max had quite a bit to say after they returned from Europe, but they aren't angry with you anymore."

"I'm certain they did. I didn't make the best impression on Mr. or Mrs. Sterling when we met." He'd already told her that. He'd already apologized to the Sterlings. Why was he babbling?

Because you want Violet and don't know how to tell her that without making an even bigger fool of yourself than you already have.

He forced himself to continue. "I'm still finding out who I am now, what I want."

"Are you considering leaving the Searchers?" Her voice held no trace of judgment, just curiosity.

"No," he replied, honestly. "But I think you and your uncle are right for changing the way the New York branch works. The way the Searchers are operating now is unsustainable. Change is going to take a long time." He forced some levity into his voice. "But it's possible."

If he could get the rest of the British Searchers to see the light. That was a big if.

~

THEY RETURNED to the hotel at daybreak, not having caught any other vampires. There was a cable from the New York branch waiting for them when they arrived, which Violet eagerly opened once they reached their room. A smile bloomed across her face as she read the contents.

"Ed and Molly Burgess are arriving this afternoon," she said. Relief poured through her at the thought of help from her friends. Well, *friend*, technically. Molly didn't do field work.

"Burgess?" Samuel said.

"Ada's brother and sister-in-law. You would've met them at the wedding." She stripped off her heavy coat and scarf, wincing as pain zinged through her sore arm. *Stupid vampire. And stupid me, for falling over.*

Samuel picked up on her discomfort immediately. "Let me take a look at that," he said. "It's been injured twice since we arrived here."

"And I told you isn't that bad." She flexed her fingers. "See? I can use it just fine.

He gave her a withering look, one she'd never seen before, that questioned her ability to tell the truth. She sighed. It wouldn't hurt to let him look at it. "Fine," she said. If he was going to insist on examining her... She started unbuttoning her blouse, noting that shoulder throbbed a little when she moved her arm just so. Her arm was tender, but not broken.

He looked a little alarmed when he saw what she was doing. "Sam," she said, "It isn't as though you haven't seen me undressed before. If you want to do an examination, you can do an examination." She shrugged out of her blouse and draped it over the back of the room's straight-backed chair.

He sucked in a harsh breath. At first, she thought it was due to nervousness or her being bold enough to take off her blouse in front of him, until she saw her reflection in the looking glass on the wall. Her arm and shoulder were a map of deep blue and purple bruises. "Oh, damn," she said, turning to the side so she could see the full extent of the damage.

"Indeed." Samuel's voice was dry. "Let me check you for sprains."

"I didn't know English lawyers studied medicine," she said, but she let him gingerly prod around her shoulder. She cringed as his fingers poked a particularly tender area, but his touch was still gentle.

A shiver coursed through her. Even if it hurt a little, she liked having his hands on her.

"We don't, but I have a basic understanding of field medicine thanks to the Searcher physicians. I assume American ones do, as well." His voice had an oddly husky quality to it, and when their eyes met in the looking glass's reflection, she thought she saw desire there.

Or she could be imagining things. He seemed strangely discomfited over their kiss on the boat.

She tried to keep their conversation professional, at least for his sake. "You're assuming correctly, and I'd be doing the same thing if our roles were reversed. Ow!" That was right over her shoulder blade. His hand stilled but didn't move from her skin. It prickled with awareness, some-

thing she was sure he picked up. She hastily contin-
ued. "But I think I'm just sore and bruised. Nothing's broken or won't heal over a few days."

His fingers drifted down her bare arm, and her breath stuttered at the contact. This time, when their gazes met in the looking glass, she could definitely see a spark of interest there, and knew hers had to be giving her own away.

She remembered that kiss. He'd been good at it. She wanted to experience that again, this time without the threat of vampires or freezing water pouring down around them. Her eyes flicked to the bed, and any exhaustion she thought she was feeling before evaporated.

She wanted to show him that life was still worth living, that what happened in London wasn't his fault. That people and organizations could change and adapt, that he wasn't a bad person. She wanted to kiss away those fears, and more.

"Breakfast," he said, snapping her out of her daydream. There was a rasp to his voice that hadn't been there before.

He's just as affected as I am.

"Beg your pardon?"

"We haven't eaten a proper meal since yesterday. Shall I have something delivered to our room?"

He was right, of course. "Yes," she said. "Just let me——"

He shook his head. "I'll handle it. I'm still presentable." He let her go, and she already missed the contact. Her skin still tingled where he'd touched her.

"Samuel, are you suggesting I'm not presentable?"

He'd already crossed the room and had his

hand on the doorknob. His gaze perused her, slow and lazy, and Violet's belly clenched in anticipation. "No," he said. "In fact, Violet, I don't think I've ever seen you look more presentable."

Her breath hitched.

Almost as quickly as he'd said the words, his expression shuttered, as if he was just as shocked at himself. He left the room without saying anything else, closing the door behind him.

Violet saw, in those seconds before and after he spoke, a hint of the man Ada told her about, who Samuel said he used to be. Not the arrogance, but a confidence he hadn't shown her thus far. She liked it.

She finished undressing and slid her night-gown over her head, wincing at the pain radiating from her arm as she did so. It would get worse before it got better, she decided, then draped a wool wrapper around her shoulders, and waited.

For what?

Samuel had kissed her once, and it was to protect their activities on the boat. He'd made *one* flirtatious remark, one that was out of character for the man she knew. There was likely nothing to look forward to, besides some breakfast.

That notion depressed her a little, and she sighed. When was the last time a man paid her any attention?

It was an easy enough question to answer: Violet had spent some time away at Smith College, beginning when she was nineteen. She'd had seven glorious months of freedom away from New York, the Searchers, and her father, before being summoned home when her father grew ill. Seven months to explore Massachusetts, a whole other world away from New York, and the ideas and people there.

Including Geoffrey Bailey, the first man she was ever besotted with and hoped to marry, until her father's illness and her obligation to the Searchers scuttled those plans. The last Violet had heard, Geoffrey married and joined the Episcopalian clergy. She had read about his push to ban automatic chapels from Boston, tiny places of worship that were already long established in New York. Violet had ducked into one or two of them herself on occasion to protect herself from vampires.

But Geoffrey Bailey wasn't here now, and truthfully, Violet hadn't given him much thought in years. For the first time in longer than she cared to remember, she felt need thrumming through her veins, along with worry that Samuel's thoughts weren't aligned with hers. His kiss and teasing aside, he was still recovering from a terrible shock.

She would wait for him to come to her, she decided.

The room's door opened and Samuel walked in holding a picnic basket. He caught her raised eyebrow and sighed. "This is all the kitchen could provide," he said. "The cook was most displeased that I asked for breakfast in my room until I explained that my wife was feeling poorly."

"And the cook agreed?"

"Begrudgingly, which is why I'm bringing everything to you in a basket rather than a servant bringing a tray." He opened the basket and set everything on the small desk pushed against the wall: a pair of small plates, cooling rashers of bacon, hardboiled eggs that Violet already knew were going to be cold, and some scones that looked fresh.

"Thank you," she said, and touched the sleeve of his coat, letting her hand linger. When she looked up at him, she thought she saw her own thoughts mirrored there.

Maybe I'm not wrong about all of this.

Still, she wasn't going to push her luck. They filled their plates, and Samuel sat down on the end of the bed. Neither said anything, but Violet wasn't sure what to say anyway.

"How's your arm?" he finally asked.

"You mean, has it worsened since you left? It's fine," she said. "I'm really all right. I'd tell you otherwise."

He seemed to accept her explanation, and they finished their meal. Violet gathered the plates and stacked them in the picnic basket, and Samuel ducked behind the screen to change into his night-clothes. Violet closed the window drapes, casting the room in near-total darkness, then slid into bed.

I'm thinking about this too much.

She was probably wrong about his feelings toward her, if he had any. She was such a fool, so lacking in affection that she was taking a kiss he'd given her under duress and letting her imagination run away with her.

Maybe I should take off my nightdress?

No, that would make things a million times worse if she was wrong.

Samuel slid into bed beside her, rustling the blankets, and his body heat immediately warmed the bed. Both of them lay there, stiff and, in Violet's case at least, uncomfortable. She knew she wouldn't be falling asleep any time soon, as much as she should, and she could tell from the rigidity of Samuel's body and his even, shallow breaths that he wasn't tired, either.

"I asked the front desk to knock on the door at one," he said in the darkness. "So we can meet Mr. and Mrs. Burgess at the airfield."

"Thank you."

More silence, and it drove Violet crazy. She couldn't go on like this until she'd asked him, at least. "Sam?"

"Yes?"

She swallowed. "Did you mean it when you said I'd never looked more presentable before?"

There was a pause, and she thought she'd misjudged him. He was reverting back to his arrogant, son-of-a-bitch persona he'd had back in London, courtesy of returning to the field and remembering that he was a decent Searcher. He was…

"Yes," he said.

Excitement thrummed through her at his answer. But to save her life, she couldn't think of a witty response. Wit and flirtation were Ada Sterling's domain, not hers. She'd spent her life hunting things and organizing others. All she could do, while she groped for words, was hope that Samuel wasn't insulted by her silence.

Finally, she summoned a response. "Thank you."

The bedclothes crumpled and Samuel turned away.

It took Violet a few seconds to realize he was laughing. "Damn it!" she said. "What's so funny?"

"You. You're adorable, Violet." He rolled on to his side to face her, and she could make out his features in the dark.

She levered herself up on her good arm, propping her head in her hand. "Thank you again, I guess," she said. "And *don't* laugh at me."

"I'm not."

"I suppose you're laughing *with* me." He didn't respond to that, but she could still see his grin. She liked it; she hadn't seen him happy at all since he landed in New York.

"Neither, I promise," he said. "It's an unexpected relief to meet people who aren't so gloomy."

"Ada mentioned London being rather gloomy." At least the parts where she wasn't with Max, but Violet kept that to herself.

"It is, and so are the Searchers. I don't think I understood how much until I left England."

"Samuel?"

"Yes?"

"Would it be adorable if I kissed you? Or would it just make things awkward between us?"

He was quiet again. *Well, there I've gone and fucked it all up.*

"It wouldn't be adorable," he said.

She felt her heart crack and a wave of mortification wash over her.

"It would be maddening," he said.

That was all the encouragement Violet needed. She closed the short distance between them, pressing her mouth to his. He immediately responded, arm locking around her and hauling her atop him. She sucked in a gasp as her injured arm throbbed but ignored it.

Samuel didn't. "Violet? Did I hurt you?"

"No," she said quickly, and kissed him again to banish any more of those thoughts away. She was fine. *Better* than fine.

Samuel's tongue swept into her mouth, sending heat straight through her body to her core. She adjusted herself, sliding down his body to straddle his hips. He moaned, his body thrusting up to grind his erection against her backside.

Another thrill shot through her, and then… uncertainty. She paused for only a second, but it was long enough for Samuel to take notice.

"Is something wrong?" His voice was a harsh whisper in the darkness, and Violet hated the concern there.

"No," she said, a little too quickly. She reached for the top buttons on her nightdress and plucked them open. His hand stilled hers, and she froze.

Am I doing something wrong?

He must have seen the question in her eyes. She could see understanding dawning in his face even in the darkened room. "Is this your first…?"

"No!" she said again. Embarrassment flooded her, replacing the desire that had been coursing through her veins just a moment ago. "Sam, kiss me again." She angled her face over his, but he turned away before her mouth could touch him. *Oh, damn.* "Did I do something wrong?"

His hands gently clasped her wrists. "Violet, I'm not upset."

She was rapidly getting there. What was the problem? She wanted him and could tell by the stiffness of his body and ragged breathing that he still wanted her. "I'm not either," she lied.

There was an understanding look on his face that tugged at her, urged her to be honest, and she didn't know which she hated more: that look, or her own ineptitude. She probably should have let him take the lead on this. "Um," she said lamely. She may as well be honest. "I thought that was what I was supposed to do," she said. "I'm sorry."

"Don't apologize," he said. "I'm just surprised you were willing to take everything off right away."

Tears sprang to Violet's eyes and she blinked them away. She prayed he didn't notice. She took a moment to compose herself, to sound like she wasn't on the verge of crying. All she could manage was, "I don't know what to say."

His fingers massaged slow circles on her wrists, the touch gentle and soothing. "I don't either, except it's been in my experience..." He cleared his throat, and briefly looked away.

This just kept getting worse and worse. "Samuel, I don't care if there were other women. I'd expect that, actually."

"It's not that."

"What is it? I thought you wanted this." There was a wobble to her voice, and she silently cursed it.

"I do, I just want this to be good for you. For both of us. Not a hurried fumbling in the dark," he said.

That made sense. Violet relaxed a little, but all the same, she slid off Samuel's hips and settled in the bed next to him. "I hadn't considered that."

"It's something you may want to."

"You're not angry?" she said, her voice small.

"Why on earth would I be angry?"

"I don't know!" She tried and failed to keep the exasperation out of her voice. "That I'm inexperienced?"

"That doesn't bother me."

"That I'm inexperienced and not a virgin?"

"I'm not a virgin, either. I wouldn't hold that against you. As I've told you, Violet, I want this to be good for you."

The absurdity of their situation finally fell over her, and she had to bite back a smile. "I'm being ridiculous, aren't I?"

"No. I'm a little confused, is all. And I imagine you are, as well."

"Yes." She may as well admit what was troubling her. "I'm not sure what to do. What you like."

"I like *you*, Violet, but I don't think that's here nor there for you right now. Men aren't a monolith any more than women are."

"I know!" God, if the events of the past ten minutes hadn't taught her that yet, then she was a bigger idiot than she thought. "Sam, can you just kiss me again already?"

He didn't offer a reply, just a scorching kiss that left her insides quivering. He moved over her, hands sliding down her body, and she felt herself relax. This was supposed to be fun and pleasurable.

She could do that.

His tongue swept into her mouth and she eagerly reciprocated, the motion drawing a small mewl from her. He took that as a sign of encouragement, his hand reaching for the hem on her nightgown and pushing it up her leg. His other hand found the small buttons marching down the front of her nightdress and he flicked one open.

She sucked in a harsh breath of surprise, and he pulled away. "All right?" he asked.

Very much so. "Yes."

He deftly unfastened a few more buttons, baring her breasts to the air. Her nipples stiffened from the temperature change and his appreciative look. His fingers traced the inside of her calf, moving up to her knee. She tried not to giggle. "Sorry," she said breathlessly. "I'm ticklish there."

"What about here?" His fingers moved up a little higher, to her thigh. She involuntarily stiffened a little against him and felt Samuel's erection press against her hip. She didn't know which felt better.

"Higher."

He obliged, his eyes never leaving hers. Part of her wanted to close hers, self-conscious at the reaction he easily coaxed from her, but another, more wanton part thrilled at the intense look on his face, a look she had managed to put there.

Her voice was a strangled whisper when she spoke. "Touch me."

She didn't elaborate, and she didn't need to. His fingers skimmed over her damp center, the space she only touched when she was home alone, under cover of darkness. Then he pushed inside her.

The motion nearly set off a chain reaction inside Violet. She hadn't expected this to be so intense, every nerve ending set on fire. Her hips moved of their own accord as Samuel slid his fingers in and out of her, her body already feeling like it was going to coil in on itself as she sought relief.

She hadn't expected to have that happen so soon.

"Samuel," she whispered in his ear, breath ragged. "I need..."

He seemed to sense what she needed. He fitted another finger in her, his tempo increasing. His mouth caught her lips, tongue tangling with hers and muffling her cry as she shattered around his hand.

She lay in his arms for a long moment, savoring the contact. Warm affection for the man next to her flowed through her, along with the distant thought that she could get used to this. Could get used to this with *him*. "I feel like I should thank you," she said.

"Thanks isn't necessary. I enjoyed that, too."

Violet could still feel the rapid beat of Samuel's heart and his cock still against her spent body. "What about you?" she asked.

"What about me?"

Shyness overcame her again, which was ridiculous, given what they'd just shared. And he *knew* what she meant, drat him; she could hear it in his voice. She parsed her words carefully. "I want you to have that, too."

"You're offering?"

She rolled her eyes. He was teasing her, and she didn't know how to respond in kind yet. "Yes, and you know that." She lowered her voice a little, trying to inject as much suggestion into it as she could. "Show me what you like."

She must have done something right, because his eyes darkened and he took her hand, placing it over the swell of his cock. She stroked it through his night clothes, hoping she didn't come across as too experimental.

Although judging from the way Samuel closed his eyes and bucked his hips slightly in response, she didn't need to worry about that. Emboldened by his reaction, she unlaced his trousers and wrapped her hand around his cock, stroking the soft skin.

He took her hand in his and firmly slid it up and down. "Like that."

She did so, and he let go of her hand and lay back against the pillows. Violet's hand slid up his length, squeezing a little at the top as he'd wordlessly instructed her to. She felt a little heady in the power that he'd just given her, the trust he'd placed in her.

"Faster," he said, his voice a strangled gasp.

She obliged, and he moaned, his body tensing under her grip. A growl finally escaped him and he came, sticky wetness coating her fingers. A thrill shot through Violet at the sight, that she could have this effect on him.

He didn't stay abed for long, though. He quickly got up and fetched a wet cloth from the washstand in the corner to clean them both off. When he came back to bed, he collected her in his arms and pressed a kiss to her temple. "Thank you."

Violet snuggled against him and threw an arm across his chest.

She could definitely get used to this.

CHAPTER

SIX

Samuel woke before Violet but didn't move to get out of bed. Instead, he watched her breathe and the slight flutter of her closed eyelids as she dreamed. There was a look of contentment, of peace, on her face that wasn't usually there when she was awake.

It was such a shame that he was leaving when the investigation was over. He couldn't remember the last time he connected with anyone, Searcher or not, in his life. Violet was special, and he was going to miss her terribly.

She stirred and her green eyes blinked, focusing on Samuel. A blush stained her cheeks. "Good morning," she said. "Afternoon. Whatever it is right now."

Samuel leaned over and kissed her. A small gasp of surprise escaped her, but she responded, the gesture heating his blood. He forced himself to break away; they had other, less enjoyable activities to take care of today, starting with meeting the Burgesses at the airfield. "We have to get out of bed," he said, regret in his voice.

"I know." Her voice betrayed her disappointment with their situation. "Let's find Lambert and start staking the rest of those vampires. It's odd that he didn't leave us a note this morning."

Samuel didn't want to think about Frederick Lambert. Or the Burgesses, for that matter, but there wasn't much choice to be had in the matter. When it came down to it, he and Violet would always put duty before pleasure. It was a depressing thought, but important if the rest of the human race didn't end up as vampire bait.

He tried to reassure her. "I'm certain Lambert is fine."

She didn't seem convinced. She crawled out of bed and shook out her hair. "I don't know, Sam. He was hunting alone in unfamiliar territory. I have a bad feeling about all of this. It's odd and out of character for him."

"I don't wish to cast blame," Samuel said, but Violet shook her head and cut him off.

"He shouldn't be hunting alone," she repeated. "I know. I don't think the Canadians have realized the gravity of the vampire problem. There used to be so few here." She blew out a frustrated sigh. "Let's get dressed and find Ed and Molly."

THE SIGHT of Edgar and Molly Burgess, waiting patiently at the same station the trolley had left her and Samuel days ago, warmed Violet's heart. She hugged each, holding on a little longer than she normally would, grateful to have some familiar people around her. Not that Samuel wasn't familiar —he certainly was now—but he left her nerves jangled in a way she'd never experienced before. Jangled nerves did not go well with being a professional vampire slayer. Besides, she missed her friends.

"Thank God you're here," Violet said by way of greeting.

"It's a little quiet in New York without Ada, so we're happy to help," Edgar said. "We came here for our honeymoon but didn't have much of a chance to see the falls."

"Ed!" Molly looked shocked at his words. Color stained her cheeks in a way that had nothing to do with the cold.

Samuel also looked a little scandalized at Edgar's remark, but didn't say anything.

Neither had much luggage, and they walked out of the trolley station toward the hotel. Afternoon sun warmed them marginally, but it was better than the bone-deep chill that permeated Niagara Falls at night. Violet appreciated the warmth, as mild as it was. "Frederick Lambert appears to have gone missing," she said. She and Samuel had sent a cable to his hotel in St. Catharines that morning and nothing came of it. She was now officially worried about him.

Edgar thought for a moment. "Canadian liaison? The name sounds familiar."

"Ada probably invited him to the wedding out of courtesy. He's from the Montreal branch. He's been hunting alone in St. Catharines since we arrived."

"Dangerous and impractical," Edgar said.

"I know." Violet hoped Lambert had simply forgotten to check in with her and Samuel, that the telegraph lines connecting Niagara Falls and St. Catharines were down, *anything*.

Do you really *believe Lambert would actually forget to check in with you?*

"How bad is the infestation?" asked Molly. "Not that I can do that much to help with it, but I like to stay informed."

Edgar's wife was only recently made aware of the existence of vampires, and since their marriage worked as a telegraph operator for the New York branch. She didn't have anything in the way of field training, and Violet knew she would be staying at the hotel while they went out hunting at night. How she could do that while Edgar worked, Violet didn't know.

"You can sense nests of newly turned vampires as we get closer to residences," Samuel said. "We staked a cellar full of them a couple of days ago. There's at least one more major one somewhere in town, and we need help to extinguish them all."

"Can you sense them?" Violet asked Edgar.

He cocked his head to the side, as if listening for them. "My sense isn't quite as strong as Ada's," he said.

"Nonsense," said Violet.

"It's not as strong as Ada's, but I'm picking it up," he said. "It feels like it's been muted somehow."

"Because they're probably all underground," Violet said.

"It's going to be a pain in the rear to track them down, then," Molly said.

"It is, and there's enough nighttime activity to keep us up at all hours," Samuel added. Violet could hear frustration in his voice.

"Let's check into that hotel," Edgar said. "Then we'll start hunting."

It wasn't going to be as simple as Edgar thought. "This is a smaller town," Violet pointed out. "Strangers don't often wander away from the falls' vicinity. People notice when strangers are skulking around their neighbors' gardens." That hadn't happened yet, aside from meeting the Graves brothers at the haunted house, but it was only a matter of time. "People are likelier to know and trust their neighbors as well."

"We'll make it work," Edgar said, determination in his voice.

They were quiet during the short walk to the hotel, although Violet noticed Edgar and Molly exchanging the occasional adoring look between them. *Newlyweds*, she thought, then remembered another couple. "How are Ada and Max? Have you heard from them?"

"She sent us a cable a couple of days ago," Edgar said. "It just said that she and Max arrived safely in Italy and the weather was lovely. That's it. I don't think either of them have been hunting while they're there."

Knowing Ada, that meant she hadn't found any to stake. She wasn't one to take a holiday if there was a vampire in her vicinity. She would have found a way to communicate that through code had she or Max found any.

Violet was relieved to hear her friend was actually enjoying some time off. She'd tried to do that, when she made that trip to Dresden last spring, and ended up chasing vampires across Europe. Of course, she'd also met Max in the process, so the holiday hadn't entirely revolved around stakes and bloodshed.

Edgar and Molly were booked in a room on the same floor as Violet and Samuel, and they waited while the other couple put their bags away. While Edgar and Samuel talked about the likeliest places to find another vampire nest that afternoon,

Molly ushered Violet into a corner on the opposite side of the room.

"How are you getting on?" she asked, her voice a whisper.

Violet was taken aback at the question, unused to personal queries about her life. But she knew Molly meant well, and it had been so long since Violet confided in anyone. Still, she chose her words carefully. "It's going well," she said.

"Violet, I'm not blind," she said. "I saw the way you two are looking at each other, and even though he'd never say anything about it to your faces, I'm certain Ed's noticed, as well."

How could she describe the whirlwind of emotions that tore through her whenever she looked at Samuel, how confusing all of that was? Violet hadn't expected to ever feel that way about anyone again, not since she'd bid *adieu* to Geoffrey Bailey all those years ago. She'd chosen duty over pleasure, and never questioned that decision until now.

And she really shouldn't be questioning that decision, anyway. She'd known Samuel for a couple of weeks. It was impossible to know if they had a future together when they'd known each other for such a short time, wasn't it?

Why are you even considering a future with a man you've barely met, Violet? You have more sense than that!

Molly was still waiting for an answer. "You don't have to tell me," she said. "Just remember that if you feel like talking about it, I'm always willing to listen."

"It's complicated," Violet said, her voice a harsh whisper. "He's a fine Searcher."

A fine Searcher who would return to London after they'd taken care of the vampire issue in Niagara Falls.

The understanding on Molly's face was her undoing, though, and after a quick, furtive glance at the men to make sure they weren't listening, she said, "I like him very much. More than I should. And that's all it should come to, really."

"You don't believe you deserve some happiness with someone else?"

When she put it that way... "It's never been something I've seriously considered," Violet said. At least not since she left college.

Before Molly could respond, Edgar spoke up. "It'll be getting dark soon," he said. "Why don't we have some supper, and then start hunting?"

Violet was relieved at the change of subject, unsure how to put her feelings into words. "Of course," she said. "Samuel, please lead on."

It wasn't quite as bitingly cold when they left the hotel to hunt, but Samuel knew that would change as night continued to fall. Violet left instructions at the front desk to refer any correspondence to Molly, who waited behind in the room she shared with Edgar. But Samuel's suspicions about Fred Lambert were growing more sinister with each minute they didn't hear from him.

The lack of communication from Lambert wasn't his only concern. Violet was too, and certainly the hurriedly whispered conversation between her and Molly gave him pause. He knew they were talking about him, and while Samuel didn't usually indulge in gossip, he was curious about what Violet told her friend. Molly and Edgar were observant, a necessary trait for successful vampire hunters, but right now that attribute put him on edge. He really needed to be more careful about not making calf eyes at her in the presence of others, if that's what he'd been doing.

Damn it, he liked her. He respected her. And he was going to miss her like hell when he went home.

He shook his head a little as if to clear away the distraction that Violet presented. He had a job to do right now, and he could not let his concentration be diverted by remembering what she tasted like, the soft noises she made when he touched her…

God damn it, Seecombe, pull yourself together!

Lambert, he reminded himself. They needed to find Lambert tonight, assuming the Canadian Searcher was still alive. Samuel immediately sobered. As much as he knew Violet hoped otherwise, he didn't have a good feeling about Lambert's disappearance.

But could he trust his intuition again? He hadn't since Radcliffe's death.

He heard a gust of wind picking up speed nearby and took a deep breath to prepare himself for it. Even so, the sensation of icy air against his face still stole the breath from his lungs. How could people tolerate these conditions?

He sneaked a glance at the others, who looked just as shocked by the cold as he was. Perhaps it wasn't just him.

CHAPTER

SEVEN

It was half past eight when the three of them sensed something nearby, an odd sensation that Violet hadn't really experienced before. She could tell that it was more than one monster somewhere in one of these dilapidated houses, but her sense felt … muted, almost. As if it had been turned down like a lamp's flame.

Samuel and Edgar wore matching confused expressions on their faces. Already guessing the answer, she said, "Can you feel that?"

"I'll be damned if I can tell why I feel like this," Edgar replied. "Never had this happen before."

Samuel pointed a gloved finger at a shuttered house. "Me, neither. I have a feeling there's something over there."

The neighborhood they'd walked to in the freezing cold was on the very edge of town, a small street where the houses looked totally abandoned. There were footprints in the snow, some of booted feet and others bare, another sure sign that vampires were nearby. She guessed that in the summers the yards would be overgrown with weeds and the whole street would look incredibly eerie, a sight that would give the city-dwelling Violet the willies. It was the kind of place conscientious parents warned their children never to play in. She was an adult, an experienced monster hunter, and she still felt the hairs on the back of her neck stand up in a way that had little to do with the cold. There was probably a group of vampires nearby, she thought, but they were a group as well. There wasn't any ice or rolling water beneath her to cause her to lose her footing today, nor was she facing this threat alone.

The house Samuel pointed to was entirely boarded up, including the front door. They checked the back of the house and found the cellar door splintered around the handle, as if someone had tried to break in, and a shiny new lock held it fast. The snow around the door had been stomped around in without having been cleared away.

Dread kept slithering down Violet's spine, and with it, the metallic taste of fear in her mouth. She had an inexplicable urge to run away, that whatever was hiding in this house was a million times worse than anything else she'd seen before.

"I think we should enter through the front door," said Samuel, not bothering to hide the uncertainty in his own voice.

Uncertainty. Not fear. Violet would not be able to bear it if he was just as afraid as she was.

Stop being frightened! Whatever's in that house, you've killed their kind before!

Edgar nodded, and Violet found herself doing the same. "We'll break in through the front door," he said. "We'll stay together, all right? It isn't safe for two of us to pair off and another to go alone."

Samuel visibly blanched at the idea, and Violet knew he was thinking about poor Radcliffe.

Edgar and Samuel easily popped off the boards nailed over the door and left them on the porch. Samuel tested the rusty doorknob, its loud squeak of protest making all of them wince.

Violet looked up and down the deserted street out of habit but didn't see anyone.

A black shape zipped across the darkening sky across the street. It grazed the rotting roofs of the houses. "Sam, Ed," Violet said urgently. "I just saw a bat."

"Damn," said Edgar. He pushed his shoulder against the doorframe. "The lock's nearly rusted out. Give me a minute." He threw all of his weight against the door and it swung open, banging against the wall.

Violet squinted at the foyer's darkness.

"Fuck!"

The voice was familiar, and Violet's stomach turned over.

Beside her, Samuel paled. "Lambert?" he said.

"It's bad." Lambert's voice sounded from somewhere on the house's first story. "It's bad in here. I did what I could, but..." His words were cut off with the sound of a body hitting the floor and a harsh cry.

All three of them burst through the foyer, following the sound of Lambert's voice. The sounds of scuffling and snarls sent Violet's heart racing. Only vampires could make those noises.

Oh, God, Frederick, what have you gotten yourself into?

A single oil lamp lit a small, empty sitting room at the back of the house, illuminating the fight playing out on the floor. Lambert, his clothes torn and bloodstained, wrestled with a naked vampire whose eyes glowed red with rage as they tussled.

His fangs were out, but he made no move to bite at Lambert's neck.

The light caught Lambert's own red-tinged eyes as they fought, and Violet nearly screamed.

"Stake him!" Lambert shouted. "*Now!* Fucking hell, do it!"

The vampire shrieked something in a language Violet didn't recognize before leaping to his bare feet. Spittle dripped from his lips as he advanced on Violet.

Despite her dawning horror, she swiftly reacted. Just as he leapt toward her, she raised her stake and mallet and neatly plunged them through his pale chest before he realized what was happening. He stumbled away from her before sliding to the dusty floor and crumbling into oily dust.

Dusty floor… Violet looked down. The greasy ash on the floor wasn't dust.

"They got me," said Lambert. "Just before dawn a couple of days ago, I think. I haven't been able to keep track of the days." His eyes hadn't lost that red hue.

It took a few seconds for Lambert's words to sink in.

They got me.

Edgar was the first to speak. "Oh, Jesus."

"I haven't eaten since I was turned," said Lambert. "And I'm hungry."

Tears welled up in Violet's eyes. "Oh, Fred…"

Lambert's eyes shone in a way that had nothing to do with vampirism. "It's a hazard of the trade," he said, trying to sound gruff. "I knew you'd come around soon. I took care of most of the nest in this house before I had to sleep the days away, and the ones across the street."

"I saw a bat before we came in," Violet said.

"There's still one floating around," Lambert said. "But I won't be one of them. I am *not* eating anyone."

"Maybe you could be treated," said Violet desperately. "We could take a dirigible to New York." A lump formed in her throat, and she had to force herself to speak over it. "You could see one of the Searchers' doctors there."

That was the awful feeling she'd had outside, that they'd all had, the sense picking up that one of their own had been turned.

"No, Violet." Lambert shook his head sadly. A blood-tinged tear slid down his cheek, and he impatiently brushed it away. "I don't have that much time before the vampire bloodlust starts and I eat someone in town. I can already feel it starting." He squared his shoulders and looked at all three of them, determination on his face. "I need a favor from one of you."

Tears leaked from Violet's eyes and she shook her own head. "No."

"I'll do it," Edgar said, stepping forward.

Lambert nodded and sized him up. "New York branch?"

"Yep. Name's Edgar Burgess."

"Pleased to meet you, Edgar. I'm Fred Lambert, out of Montreal." He held out a hand, which Edgar looked surprised to see before he shook it. "You seem a decent fellow for someone who's going to be my executioner."

Lambert looked at Violet, who had let Samuel wrap his arms around her. "Violet, Seecombe, let the Montreal branch know as soon as possible. Tell them the problem near the border was much worse than any of us thought, and I'm a goddamned fool for not bringing along a partner. That undead bastard flying around outside will be close by, and as far as I can tell he's the last one on this street. I staked the ones in the cellar." He looked at Edgar. "We need to get this over with as soon as possible. You're all starting to smell good."

A sob escaped Violet, and she pressed her face into Samuel's coat.

"Do you need help?" Samuel asked Edgar quietly, his voice a rumble under Violet's ear.

"I'm not going to fight back," Lambert said. "I think it's best if you escorted Violet out, though."

Violet raised her face to look at Lambert for the last time, noticing now that he had tiny fangs that extended over his bottom lip. There was a hungry look in his eyes that chilled her to her soul.

Frederick Lambert was fighting with a new, demonic side now, and losing.

"Goodbye, Fred," she said.

"It was a pleasure knowing you and your family," he said. "Pleasure to work with you as well, Seecombe."

She let Samuel guide her out of the room to the hallway, and he closed the door behind them. She noticed that he still held on to his stake and mallet, ready to jump back in the room should Edgar require help.

But all Violet heard was Edgar's murmured apologies and the sickening sound of a wooden stake plunging into flesh, followed by a strangled noise of pain. After a blood-curdling half-second, the unmistakable sound of a body hit the floor.

The ensuing silence was so loud Violet could hear her own heartbeat pulsing through her body, thought she could hear Samuel's, as well.

The door opened, and Edgar slipped out. "We need to get out of this house now," he said. "I knocked over the oil lamp to destroy the evidence. This whole house is going to be a death trap in about five minutes."

"Frederick?" said Violet.

"He went peacefully," said Edgar, his voice curt. But Violet could hear the pain there. "And staking a fellow Searcher was the worst goddamn thing I've ever had to do. Let's go."

~

THAT BLOODY BAT still circled the street when they let themselves out of the house, mocking all of them. "Get down here!" Violet screamed into the night. "Show yourself, you fucking bastard!"

Samuel's heart broke for her, but he didn't have time to console her over the loss of her friend right now. He and Edgar stood at the ready, stakes and mallets out, Edgar's still dusty from executing Lambert. The moon overhead offered just enough light so they could see the footprints in the snow.

The smell of smoke descended on the small group as it seeped from the windows of the old house behind them. Whether they found that vampire or not, very shortly they would have to leave. Fire had a way of attracting attention, and they would not be able to explain away their weapons.

The bat flopped down on the snow and shifted into a nude, pale-skinned woman, tangled hair streaming behind her in the winter wind. An inhuman snarl escaped her, and she launched herself at Violet.

Violet nimbly jumped out of the way, and Edgar removed a small vial of holy water from his coat pocket. Uncorking it, he threw it at the creature, who screamed as it burned her skin. She hunched over in the snow, frantically scratching at her burned shoulders and back.

Violet took the opportunity to plunge her stake into the vampire's back. She slammed her mallet down with more force than Samuel had ever seen, rage marking her own features as she did. "You *bitch!*"

The vampire collapsed into the snow, the stake sticking out of her ribs. Her body began to disintegrate, and Violet retrieved her stake, pressing a booted foot on the creature's rotting back for purchase. Her heel slid into the rapidly decomposing flesh and lifted out with an audible squish.

She gave the corpse a harsh kick, scattering ashes across the snow. "That was for Fred," she said, dragging her coat's sleeve across her eyes.

The sound of breaking glass behind them had all three of them turning around. The fire was rapidly consuming the old house, having blown off the nailed-on boards and the window glass at the front.

"We need to leave now," Samuel said, reaching for Violet. She remained rooted to the spot, staring at the greasy mess that used to be a vampire. The ashes were already starting to swirl in the wind.

"Violet?" said Edgar. "He's right. We have to go before someone sees us."

She finally looked up, eyes meeting Samuel's. "All right," she said.

There wasn't any time to be sentimental about what had just happened. The three of them broke into a run, the smell of smoke in their nostrils, ashes of the house and executed vampires clinging to their clothes.

EIGHT

Two vampire-free nights in Niagara Falls had everyone convinced that the problem there had been resolved, although it was undoubtedly temporary. Vampires were expanding their ranks at a speed far faster than Violet had ever considered possible, thanks to railways and air travel. It was only bound to get worse.

A reprieve from vampires was one to enjoy while it lasted in Edgar's eyes. Since their declaration of the town being vampire-free, Edgar and Molly had remained holed up in their hotel room, with strict orders to be left alone unless a vampire-related emergency cropped up. Violet couldn't be upset with Edgar over his putting Lambert's death in the back of his mind. He had a lot to live for, a lot of people he loved.

Violet knew that Searchers occasionally died at the fangs of vampires, but she'd never been witness to it, let alone a Searcher being successfully turned. She, and everyone else in the American and Canadian branches, mourned Frederick Lambert even though the exact details of his death weren't yet widely known.

He had been brave, asking for execution. Violet had never experienced bloodlust herself, of course, but she'd witnessed it in vampires before she killed them. Lambert had been in its throes since he was turned and by his sheer force of will had managed to control it. Edgar had staked him before he could do any harm.

Violet didn't know if she was more relieved that Edgar had taken care of Lambert, or ashamed that she couldn't do it herself. She was the only person out of their small group who'd been acquainted with him, and she'd let him down.

A different kind of tiredness had enveloped her since that awful night, and she knew it would be a long time before she could process what had happened and move on. Lambert was to her as Bert Radcliffe had been to Samuel, she supposed. Physically, she was alert, as if her body had been connected to a live wire and woken up from a deep sleep. It was odd and rather disconcerting, considering how little of it she had had recently. The way she felt now could only be described as bone-deep mental exhaustion, combined with grief and feeling like she was in over her head. She was wholly unsuited to her new position with the Searchers. Violet had been proverbially burning the candle at both ends for too long and couldn't do it any longer.

With another night left in Niagara Falls before they were scheduled to return home, she realized she couldn't spend any more time rattling through the hotel room. She needed to get out. Samuel's expression was still haunted whenever she looked at him, and she thought he might need a distraction, too. Both of them lay in bed, fully dressed, staring at the ceiling, with hardly a word spoken between them for what felt like hours. She turned her head. "Do you want to see the hot air balloons?"

He shifted to look at her, the mattress dipping under his weight. She thought he might say no as his dark gaze searched her face. "Why not?"

Half an hour later, Violet and Samuel leaned against a safety rail that overlooked the river, watching the colorful balloons drift in the night sky in front of the roaring falls. He placed a proprietary hand on the small of her back, and Violet moved a little closer to him.

Such a dear man.

She knew the trauma caused by his friend Radcliffe's death had spurred changes in him, transforming him from the arrogant bastard Ada Sterling had to deal with in London to the quiet and more sensitive man that he was now. She couldn't help but feel guilty for being pleased that *this* was the man she had come to know, when the reasons for his change had been so awful.

But Violet had changed too, since seeing one of her friends and allies turned into what they all hated the most. Frederick Lambert's death would have the same impact on her as Radcliffe's on Samuel, would change her in similar ways. As she watched her breath come in white puffs in the cold night air, she decided that as soon as she returned to New York, she would be resigning her lieutenant position, effective immediately. She would return to fieldwork full-time and do as much as she could to atone for Lambert's death.

She wasn't a shell of the woman she was right before Lambert's execution, but seeing his fangs and red eyes, seeing him struggle against that primal urge to eat her, had irrevocably changed her. She would not return to New York the same person.

"You seem distracted," Samuel said in her ear.

She shivered, but it wasn't from the cold. "The balloons are beautiful."

He gave her a look that clearly asked if she questioned his intelligence.

"I was thinking," she said. She didn't need to elaborate. She didn't want to talk about Lambert or the changes that would be coming to Searcher headquarters when she returned to New York.

He seemed to sense that and didn't prod further. Instead, he wrapped an arm around her and pulled her closer. Welcoming his heat, she leaned into him, his coat and scarf grazing her cheek.

The contact, innocent as it was, still brought a flush to Violet's face and a wave of heat coursing through her body. She remembered that interlude in the hotel room and every cell in her body urged her to tell Samuel to forget the hot air balloon show and go back, right now.

Was she actually brave enough to offer an indecent proposal to him? She worried her lower lip with her teeth, considering everything.

They were attracted to each other. She knew that even though Samuel hadn't tried to so much as kiss her since Lambert died. He was giving her space, just as she'd given it to him following his guilty confessions about his friend Radcliffe.

A brightly colored hot air balloon drifted past them, then floated toward the ever-rushing falls. It was fascinating to see them so closely, but Violet's initial curiosity gave way to something—*someone* —else.

In a couple of days, they would return to New

York, and from there, Samuel would go back to London.

Excitement and nervousness thrummed through her veins, each clamoring for her attention. Would he reject her?

The worst thing he can do is say no, she reminded herself.

Which meant that the best thing he could do was say yes. She took a deep breath and steeled herself. How did one go about seducing someone, anyway?

"Sam?" she said.

"Mm?"

His breath ruffled the wisps of hair that had managed to escape from underneath her hat. She could feel it even over the pervasive chill in the air.

Here goes nothing. "Do you...?" Her voice dropped off, and she took a deep breath and tried again. "Do you want to go back to the hotel?"

"We only just arrived. What for?"

Oh, God. She should have asked someone for advice. Ada, perhaps. But Ada was on the other side of America. Violet was *not* a seductress, damn it all.

She looked up at him. "I just thought... we've seen the balloons. You might want to go back to the hotel." She tried to inject as much flirtatiousness into her voice as she could and was probably failing at it.

But it seemed to work. Under the bright light offered by the streetlamp, his eyes widened. "*Oh.*"

"I just thought—we're going back home in a couple of days anyway..."

He grasped her hand and led her back through the throngs of spectators. "You don't have to talk me into it."

"I don't?" Relief poured through Violet, followed by excitement. She hadn't botched this.

"Of course not. Violet, you could talk me into anything."

Before she could form a response, his mouth crashed down on hers. In those few seconds, she forgot all about the people around them, the cold, the devastating loss the Searchers had experienced. There was only her and Samuel.

The sound of a throat indignantly clearing had him pulling away from her, and he quickly grasped her gloved hand. "Come on," he said, an uncharacteristically mischievous twinkle in his eye.

She easily kept up with his long strides as they wove their way through the crowd back to the hotel. Already her clothes felt too constricting.

She was nearly shaking when they finally reached their room, her fingers fumbling when she unwound her scarf and took off her coat. Samuel shucked his off more quickly and took over. "Here," he said, deftly unfastening the buttons.

As soon as her coat was off, he collected her in his arms and pressed a kiss to her lips that left her knees weak. She clung to his shoulders as he picked her up bodily and gently set her down on the bed, then lay next to her. Before she could move for him again, he pulled her on top of him so her legs straddled his hips, lacing her fingers through his and pulling her down for a kiss.

She could feel the hard ridge of his erection between their layers of clothes, and she'd never been more eager to take hers off. Or his, for that matter. She broke the kiss long enough to reach for the buttons on his shirt and plucked at them, far less shakily than she had with her own coat.

She didn't have much time left with him. Her

heart lurched at their inevitable separation, but she forced that thought from her mind. Violet was going to enjoy every second she still had with Samuel.

Maybe it didn't have to end after this.

But if it does... She wanted this, one sweet, selfish memory to hang on to when he returned to his starched life in London, and her to her tangled one in New York.

She pushed the sides of his shirt away to reveal his chest, with its healed scars and bite wounds from long-ago vampire hunts. She didn't care. She had her own scars. All monster hunters did.

He brushed an escaped lock of silver hair away from her face. "This won't be the only time," he said.

Her heart fluttered at those words. "What do you mean?"

"This doesn't end here," he said. "Whether I come to New York or you come to London—I need you in my life, and I've never needed anyone before. I thought it would scare me, but..." A smile bloomed across his face. "It doesn't."

"What are you saying?" Violet asked.

She had a fairly good idea what he was saying, but she wanted to be sure.

"I think I'm in love with you," he said, matter-of-factly.

His words echoed in Violet's ears. Heat flooded her body. "Really?" she said, her voice breathless.

"I wanted to tell you before I left, and now... before this," he said.

"Samuel, I'm a sure thing."

She could tell he was trying to resist rolling his eyes at that statement. "Even if you weren't, that wouldn't change anything." His thumb traced the outline of her lips. "Tell me we have a chance after we go home."

"Yes," she said. "We do. We'll make it work out, somehow."

His hands pulled at her shirtwaist buttons. "How attached are you to this blouse?"

She shrugged. "It's just a blouse. I have others at home."

"Good." His hands tore at the fabric, scattering tiny buttons across the bedclothes.

A thrill ran through Violet at the motion, and heat coiled low in her belly. She lifted herself off him just enough so she could reach for the fastening on his trousers, and he helped her push them down his body.

He slid his arms out of his shirt and tossed that aside, as well, then his underclothes. He was magnificent, all lean and corded muscle from years of fighting.

And winning. That was important to remember. Both of them had fought and come out the winners.

It was a curious and powerful feeling, being mostly-dressed with a naked Samuel Seecombe beneath her. She liked it.

He caught her appreciative look and stretched out. "Like what you see?"

"You know I do."

"I don't like being the only person on this bed in the altogether, Violet."

She was the one on top, the one who still wore most of her clothes, but there was a commanding note in his voice that told her she wasn't in charge. The notion was exciting.

"I need some help with my skirt," she said.

"Are you very fond of that skirt, Violet?"

"Are you going to rip it off me, too?"

"Would you mind if I did?"

She shook her head. "No."

He tugged at the cloth, tearing at the buttons on the back. He took more care with her corset, but still quickly unhooked it and tossed it off the side of the bed. Violet slipped out of her underclothes before he could tear them off her, as much as she wanted him to, and finally rested against him, skin-to-skin. His breath had sped up to match her own, their hearts beating in tandem.

Her responsibilities evaporated from her mind, along with grief and uncertainty—no matter what Samuel wanted for their future—just to focus on the man beneath her, the first person she'd ever shared such a connection with.

Violet's hand strayed between them and wrapped around his cock, eliciting a moan from him. She didn't stop, sliding up and down the way she knew he liked. "If you keep that up, it'll be over before it can start," he said.

Before she could form a response, he grabbed her hips and swiftly flipped her over on the bed so she was flat on her back. He kissed a warm trail down her body, then eased her knees apart to plant one between her legs.

She thought she might scream in surprise, but all that came out from her was a mewl. Her hands fisted in his hair as he lashed her with his tongue, then slid two fingers in her, thrusting them in and out of her the way he had their first time together, only this was so much more frustrating. She needed more than fingers.

Samuel seemed to sense that, and he lifted his head and crawled up the bed, his body aligning with hers. He fitted himself in the cradle of her hips, cock against her inner thigh. His mouth found hers as he fitted himself inside her, and she stiffened a little at the invasion. She forced herself to relax as he moved farther inside her, and wrapped her legs around his hips, urging him to sink deeper inside.

She could tell he was struggling to control himself with his first few, careful strokes and she wiggled her hips, urging him on. "You won't break me," she whispered in his ear.

That was all the encouragement he needed. He thrust harder inside her, increasing his pace, hips slamming against hers. She dug her nails in the scarred skin of his back as the first wave of orgasm washed over her, the intensity tearing a wail from her. She sank her teeth into Samuel's shoulder to muffle the sound, and he groaned in response, his body furiously pumping in and out of hers. He stiffened as his own climax overtook him and she felt him pulse deep within her.

He sagged against her, then rolled on his side, taking her with him. He pressed a kiss to her forehead and finally pulled out of her before drawing the bedsheet around them.

They lay together, limbs entangled, feeling the other's' heartbeats. Violet thought she could stay like this forever.

She was starting to doze off in his arms before he finally spoke. "Violet?"

"Mm?" She rearranged her arm around his chest.

"I've never been so glad to be bitten in my life."

NINE

Three months later

Angus Singer had not been pleased about Violet's resignation.

Still, to his everlasting credit, he didn't berate her too badly for stepping down. "It was bound to happen," she told him at branch headquarters. "We both knew this was temporary. Francis Burgess would be a better choice, anyway. He's literate, experienced, and his wife doesn't want him in the field anymore."

She had other ideas for how she could help improve the Searchers' fight against vampires, spurred by letters and telegrams she'd exchanged with Samuel.

Violet was pleased to find out that their affair hadn't ended with his return to London, that he hadn't just brushed off their time together as a diversion. Although even if he had, Violet wouldn't have hated him for it. Knowing that he still cared about her from his home, hundreds of miles away, warmed her heart in a way she'd never experienced before.

They also discussed in their letters the growing

problem of the lack of Searchers in Britain. That issue, accompanied by Samuel's letters and a telegram from the London branch, were the biggest reasons Violet now stood before her uncle in his office with a new announcement to make.

"I'm going to England," she said as he read a letter from Samuel explaining the issues his branch was coping with. Samuel had even included all of the photographs he'd snapped at Ada and Max's wedding. They would be happy to receive them, when Violet called on them later in the day to tell them her news.

Angus didn't reply, only reading silently. She fidgeted with her skirt while she waited.

Finally, he laid it on his desk and removed his spectacles, letting them rest against him from a thin chain around his neck. He sighed and leaned back in his chair. "I see," he finally said after a long pause.

She didn't reply.

"I shouldn't be surprised," he said. "And I'm not, really. London has a lot of work ahead of itself if it isn't going to be completely overrun by vampires within the next ten years. I know it's bad all around."

She nodded.

"You understand that you're walking into the lions' den, don't you?"

"I know," she said. "Ada and Max Sterling have told me all about the Searchers there."

"I don't know if they can offer a subjective opinion, given that Max didn't become a Searcher until he arrived in New York and Ada only dealt with them briefly."

"It's funny that you would remind me of that," Violet said. "Especially since Ada was treated terribly until she was nearly maimed. I know exactly what I'm getting myself into, and it needs to be done soon as possible. They have to expand their ranks, and they need a fresh perspective. New eyes, you know."

"I do." Weariness etched itself into Angus's features and he rubbed his eyes. "Damn it, Violet, I don't want you to go."

"I know. But you also know that New York will do fine without me. We have the best group of vampire hunters in the world. Think of me as going overseas to teach."

"Don't think I don't know that Samuel Seecombe figures into this."

"Of course he does." What was the point in denying it? Angus wasn't stupid; he knew they had been in contact since their return from Niagara Falls. Ada had breathlessly asked after him every time she received a cable or letter. While she didn't speak of their interludes in Niagara Falls to anyone save her—and even then, she was vague—she was sure it was obvious to anyone that she was in love with the man. "I'm needed in London, Angus. The vampire problem is only going to spread here if we don't extinguish it as soon as possible." She paused. "I've already purchased a dirigible ticket. It's one-way."

"What about your flat?"

"You can use it to host guests when they visit. Or who knows, maybe down the line we'll return to New York."

"You said 'we.'"

"I did."

"You're sure about this, Violet?"

"Yes," she said. "More than I've ever been of anything."

IT TURNED out that transatlantic travel was deathly boring once the novelty of flying over water wore off. And it was *cold.* A frigid Canadian or New York winter had nothing on standing on the open observation deck of a dirigible, even in April. Violet had to stay below deck for the entire flight, counting down the minutes until the vessel landed in London. Ordinarily someone who didn't mind small children, she found their bored chatter and wails in the passenger lounge nearly unbearable.

Or maybe it was the frustration of having to wait to see Samuel again. Somehow, those last few hours of waiting were worse than the months that had passed.

And beneath all of that, there was nervousness she hadn't been expecting. She'd never been so consumed by "what-ifs" in any of her travels, none of which had been farther away than Canada until now. She didn't know she was afraid of open water until she took a short, freezing trip up to the observation deck, nor did she know that she hated small spaces until she tried to rest in her cramped cabin, so small there was only room for a bed that reeked of pipe smoke. She'd never been afraid of a dirigible crashing until now, either. So she waited in the lounge, ignoring the other passengers as best she could, until the vessel docked in London.

It was early evening and her body felt out of sorts with the time shift when she finally disembarked the dirigible, a porter having hauled her trunk for her. She sat down on it to wait. A strange combination of nervousness and excitement had her stomach twisted into knots.

Despite his letters and cables, would Samuel still care for her, once they were in closer quarters?

Was she making the biggest mistake of her life, moving to England?

You can go back, she reminded herself. Although as she sucked in a deep breath of damp air, its taste so different from New York's, and saw the grand old buildings gracing what she could see of the skyline, she wasn't sure she wanted to.

You're being foolish, she chided. *You've been here all of ten minutes. You haven't seen anything or anyone of London yet.*

Or was she being foolish making this journey to help an organization that shunned women even though they could sense vampires, too? Or that she was here, largely in part, to be with a man she knew mostly through letters and telegrams?

Her thoughts were interrupted by a familiar voice calling her name. She turned, heart in her throat, to face a grinning Samuel. He held out his arms, and before she could overthink it, she ran to him.

They immediately wrapped around her and she squeezed him as tightly as she could, breathing in his familiar scent.

"I missed you," he said into her hat, knocking it askance.

"I missed you, too," she said. To her embarrassment, she realized her eyes were wet.

"I can't believe you're here."

"Me neither." She lifted her gaze to meet his. "This is lunacy, isn't it?"

"Yes, for both of us." A deliberate, polite cough had Violet turning around to face the porter, who looked slightly embarrassed at their affection in public. She dismissed him and he took off, leaving her trunk beside her.

Samuel relaxed his hold on her and gestured to a pair of men standing behind him. "This is Dr. Pilcher and Reginald. Pilcher was the doctor who sewed up Mrs. Sterling last year. Pilcher, Reginald, this is Miss Violet Singer, former second-in-command of the New York branch."

"New York extends its gratitude to you, sir."

"How are Mr. and Mrs. Sterling faring?"

"You mean, how is Max handling living in Brooklyn? He's fine. They both are. Mrs. Sterling will be earning her pilot's license shortly." Although she doubted either of them wanted to return to England any time soon, but she didn't mention that.

Reginald collected Violet's trunk and they walked through the crowded airfield to find a steam cab. They were much cleaner than she was used to, and more spacious even though the four of them shared the space.

"Did you make a hotel reservation?" Pilcher asked casually.

"No," said Violet and Samuel simultaneously.

Pilcher raised a bushy eyebrow at that answer.

"I have a room prepared for her at my home," Samuel said, and Violet's heart sank a little. But that answer seemed to mollify Pilcher a little.

The steam cab left Pilcher and Reginald at an ordinary-looking house in a working class neighborhood. He whispered in her ear so the driver couldn't hear. "That's Searcher headquarters. We'll go there tomorrow, after you've had some rest."

The cab left Samuel and Violet in front of a large home in a much grander area that reminded her of her uncle Angus's but more... stately, she supposed. Definitely older and more elegant. The driver carried Violet's trunk to the door, and a liveried servant quickly brought it inside. "Where shall I take this?" he asked Samuel.

Servants in livery. *Oh, my.*

"My bedroom," Samuel said. A thrill coursed through her at his statement. "And you will see to anything else that Miss Singer requires."

"Of course."

"Has supper been prepared?"

"In the dining room as you asked."

Samuel helped Violet out of her coat. "Are you hungry?"

She hadn't known until he asked that she was. She hadn't eaten anything aboard the dirigible, convinced that it might come back up. "Yes."

He escorted her through the house until they reached a dining room, already set. Samuel dismissed a waiting servant and pulled out a chair for Violet, then sat down next to her at the head of the table.

He lifted the cover from a silver platter, revealing a roasted chicken. "Will this suit?"

Why was he being so formal? She nodded, feeling a little confused over the whole situation. One minute he was flirtatious, the next as stiff as the day they first met.

He poured wine for both of them, and they ate in companionable silence. Despite her reservations about Samuel, she was still famished, and finished every morsel of food.

Finally, she couldn't stand it anymore. "Sam?"

"Yes?"

"Is something wrong? You're so quiet."

He paused. "No. I've just never done this before." Before she could ask for clarification, he continued. "I haven't lived with anyone, let alone someone who traveled across the ocean to be with me and help out a group of men more stubborn than I am. This is all new for me."

Relief spread through Violet at this admission. "Me, too."

"There's also the issue that I want to do unspeakable things to you right now, but as with our living arrangements, I'm unsure of the etiquette involved."

She felt her face heat at his words. "What etiquette? I wouldn't object if you carried me to your bedroom right now."

He raised an eyebrow at her and rose to his feet. Before she knew what happened, he collected her in his arms and carried her out of the dining room to the corridor, passing a scandalized servant as they did so.

She held on to him as he carried her up a set of carpeted stairs and down another long corridor to a darkened bedroom. Without setting her down he turned on a flameless candle, casting yellow light over the room.

He gently lay her down on top of a large bed and climbed in next to her. Instead of ravishing her like his eyes wordlessly promised to do in the dining room, he threaded his fingers through hers and finally kissed her.

She'd been waiting for that since he left on the dirigible back to London so many weeks ago. Her free hand reached for his shirt buttons, but he stilled it and broke the kiss.

"Is it all right that you're staying with me?"

"You already asked me that, and I said yes." She reached for him again, but he still held her off.

"I want you to stay forever, Violet."

That knot of doubt that had twisted itself in her since she boarded the dirigible unwound. She breathed a sigh of relief she hadn't known she'd been holding. "I do, too."

"You haven't seen anything of London yet, nor met the other Searchers."

"I know they're going to be challenges."

"They're willing to cooperate with you. We all know the importance of changing the old ways." He winced. "Damn it, I'm really making a muddle of all this."

What was he talking about? "No, you aren't."

"I am. I'd planned to ask you to marry me properly, not like this."

Surprise had her sitting upright. "What?"

"I'd planned on something more romantic."

"I don't need romance!" Excitement thrummed through her. She'd been hoping for this, certainly, just as much as she wanted to help extinguish the growing vampire problem. "Samuel, I'm here for you. I love you."

"I love you, too. And you deserve a proper marriage proposal, not a botched mention of one before I get you naked and have my way with you."

"Either works for me."

He turned on his side to face her, levering himself up on one arm. "Will you marry me?"

"Of course!"

"Even though I'm not on bended knee and your ring is locked in a safe in my study at the moment?"

"Yes, Sam. I already told you yes." Her fingers lightly traced his face, skimming over his jawline and the lips she loved to kiss. "We're in this together."

"For better and for worse."

"Yes." She squealed as he hauled her bodily atop him. She swore she could feel her heartbeat synchronize with his through their layers of clothing. Their breaths quickened, and his eyes darkened. "Samuel, I came here with the intention of staying. I love you."

He pressed a heady kiss to her mouth that sucked the breath from her. "I love you, too, Violet."

About the Author

Jessica Marting is a sci-fi and paranormal romance author, art enthusiast (not quite an artist, despite all that time in art school), an avid reader, and makeup collector. She lives in Toronto.

Sign up for her newsletter at jessicamarting.com/newsletter for pre-order alerts, sales, freebies, and more.

Also by Jessica Marting

Magic & Mechanicals

Wolf's Lady

Sea Change

Bound in Blood

Dragon's Keep

Spellbound

Zone Cyborgs

Haven

Paradise

Oasis

Safe Harbor

Sanctuary

Refuge

The Commons

Supernova

Celestial Chaos

The Searchers

Blood Ties

Blood Moon

Blood Virtue

Standalone Novels & Novellas

Spindle's End

Trade Secrets

Neon Vice

Dead Ringer

Escape From Europa 10

Castaways

Demon's Favor

Her Purrfect Match

www.ingramcontent.com/pod-product-compliance
Lightning Source LLC
Chambersburg PA
CBHW021733190726
48288CB00009B/3024